Watching The Dead

Jo Wolfe Psychic Detective

Book 3

Wendy Cartmell

ISBN: 9798653963544

© Wendy Cartmell 2020

Wendy Cartmell has asserted her rights under the Copyright, Design and Patents Act, 1988, to be identified as the author of this work.

This is a work of fiction. References to real places, real people, events, establishments, organisations, or locations, are intended only to provide a sense of authentication, and are used fictitiously. All other characters, incidents and dialogue are drawn from the author's imagination and are not to be construed as real.

All rights reserved.
Costa Press

By Wendy Cartmell

Sgt Major Crane crime thrillers
Deadly Steps
Deadly Nights
Deadly Honour
Deadly Lies
Deadly Widow
Hijack
Deadly Cut
Deadly Proof

Emma Harrison Mysteries
Past Judgement
Mortal Judgement
Joint Judgement

Crane and Anderson crime thrillers
Death Rites
Death Elements
Death Call
A Grave Death
A Cold Death

Supernatural Mysteries
Gamble with Death
Touching the Dead
Divining the Dead
Watching the Dead
Waking the Dead

For Holly
You keep me going.
Thank you!

Prologue

The Book of Enoch Chapter 9

'And they have gone to the daughters of men on the earth and have had sex with the women, and have defiled themselves and revealed to them all kinds of sins.'

CHAPTER 1

9 months ago...

Sat high above Chichester, clinging to the Cathedral wall, the Watcher was as good as his name. He was watching the comings and goings of the people in the city. One of those faces rarely seen, but always watching. For no one ever looked up. They should. For there was a tumult of gargoyle monsters, watching. All seeing, inspecting, searching. It was said that gargoyles were evil beings banished from the house of God. And so they were set in stone, looking outward, away from the place they really wanted to be in, but were never allowed to enter.

    The Watcher looked for all the world like a gargoyle. He was the colour of old stone worn away by time and weather. He was still; transfixed on the people far below. The only part of him that moved was his eyes. They were coal black, cold and brooding. His hands and feet had striking matching talons, large hooked nails that were both ugly and frightening. His facial expression vexed, as he cast around for suitable victims.

    Finally he found one, late in the day when the sun was

setting, and the darkness of the night was drawing in. A beautiful young girl dressed to titillate man's desires. Her long black boots covered her knees. She had black fishnet tights on, which were torn in places. Her skirt was so short you could see her buttocks. She struck him as vulnerable as she tottered along on her high heels. Alone and already inebriated. Perfect.

His laser-like eyes homed in on her and watched as she sauntered along the street, into Chichester's city centre, where the bars and clubs were filling up. Loud music filtered down to the cathedral, a thumping bass that drew the clients in. He would keep his eye on her and when she was vulnerable, he would strike. Or rather his acolyte would strike, and then the Watcher would take over the man's body and use it as his own.

It was getting more and more difficult to find suitable victims, though. Suitable victims who would do as he wanted. Become impregnated and then keep the baby. Too much of the world was changing, attitudes were hardening, women were not who they used to be. In the past, an unmarried pregnant woman would have been sent into hiding in another part of the country, or to visit distant relatives even, where they would carry the baby to full term. Then, after the birth, at best they kept the child, or worst, placed it up for adoption. Either option was good with the Watcher, he would keep an eye on his offspring until they were of an age to join him in his quest; building an army of Watchers, half human and half God, who would rule the world with an iron fist, for millennia.

But now? Now, women were far more in control of their own lives and their own bodies. Much more attuned to them than they were before. Harder in attitude and less likely to care what anyone thought of them. Less the distressed maiden and more 'It's my body and I'll do what I want with it', feminist. Which usually resulted in them aborting the unwanted foetus. This was deeply frustrating to the Watcher. It made him angry, unstable, liable to lash out when thwarted.

Still, it was his lot to carry on. To find women, to get them pregnant, then hope. For surely the law of averages meant that a few would keep the babies. He guessed he would have to keep trying, if he was to have any chance of building an army of offspring.

As the cloak of the night settled on him, the Watcher closed his eyes and concentrated, cast around until he found the mind of the man he was seeking. His message was simple. It was time to party.

CHAPTER 2

9 months ago…

Abbey groaned. Bloody hell, not again. She had the hangover from hell. Her head was pounding, she felt sick and she had absolutely no recollection of what had happened the night before. How had she got home? Had anyone come back with her? By that she meant a man. There were odd flashes of memory. Of dancing. Of catching the eye of a rather fit bloke. But after that… nothing. No matter how hard she tried to remember. Not that that was unusual. If anyone liked to party, it was Abbey. She opened her eyes. Jesus that sun was strong. Struggling up, she swung her legs off the bed and immediately wished she hadn't. As she sat there swaying, a worm of an idea burrowed its way into her brain. She had to change her ways. There had to be a better way of living than this.

If she was honest with herself, Abbey the party animal, was finding her life rather dull and tarnished, not the super shiny exciting one that it used to be. She'd got into the habit of partying all weekend, only to find that the hangovers now lasted days instead of hours. By mid-week she'd just about recovered, only to gear up for Friday night once again. She realised she hadn't worked in months. She was trying, and failing, to live on benefits and relying more and more on the charity of her friends for drugs and tobacco. Oh and she was shoplifting to feed herself. Mustn't forget that nugget.

She staggered to the loo, avoiding the mirror. She knew what she'd find there and couldn't face it; bloodshot eyes, dull skin, spots, the remnants of her make up plastered over her face, mascara ground into her eye lids and patchy lipstick still staining her lips. Not to mention her hair. Her blond tresses were matted and greasy. And she was so thin she was starting to look emaciated. No regular food, too much alcohol. Drugs to keep her up and then to put her to sleep, wasn't a recipe for a healthy life.

Close to throwing up, she banged her way off door frames and furniture, back to bed, closed her eyes and waited for blessed oblivion to claim her.

If Abbey had looked in the mirror, she would have found someone else, or something else, staring back at her. Watching over her shoulder. Staying close. Keeping its eye on her. And although she didn't know it just yet, she wouldn't be on her own again. For she was under the spell of the Watcher.

It was a whole two days later when Abbey felt able to get up and stay up. She'd tried before but given up after going to the loo. It appeared that she was experiencing the worst hangover she'd ever had.

Her dreams were plagued with strange and horrible sights. It was as though she'd taken LSD and was in the clutches of dreamscapes and nightmares. Everything was distorted, everything good morphed into horrible and all her friends dead or dying.

Dancing in clubs, opposite mates who turned into zombies, or skeletons, or ghosts before her very eyes. Flesh melting away, clothes tattered and torn, open mouths containing things other than teeth, things that moved and wobbled and slithered. Smells that made her nausea worse. She gagged and tried to swallow down the bile but couldn't. As she threw up, she woke, shivering and sweating.

24 hours later, the splitting headache had gone, helped by the copious amounts of water she'd drunk and the pain killers she'd managed to keep down. She sat on the side of her bed, trembling and weak and managed to take her make up off at last. Then she headed for the shower, enjoying the warm spray sloughing off the dried perspiration. She washed and conditioned her hair, then turned the water to cold to wake her up. The shock did the trick and she emerged shaking and shivering but feeling more alive than she had in days, if not weeks. Actually it was months if she was honest with herself. Looking in the mirror she found her eyes and skin clear, her hair squeaky clean and her hunger sharp.

As she looked away, she thought she caught sight of something in the mirror, standing behind her. Something black and pulsing and menacing, seen from the corner of her eye. She whirled around but found it was only her dressing gown hanging from the hook on the back of the door. She laughed, but there was no mirth in it. It was from fear, a release of tension.

Quickly leaving the bathroom and returning to her room, she was struck by how musty it smelled. Once dressed in the only miss- matched clean clothes she could find, Abbey flung open the curtains and released the latch on the window. As she pushed it open, she could smell the flowers outside and hoped their scent would pervade her room, banishing the sickly unwashed smell. She then made her way to the kitchen in the shared house she lived in. What to eat? Dry toast as she had no butter? But then she spied a lone avocado lurking in the back of the vegetable drawer in the fridge. That would do, after all avocados were super foods, weren't they? Toasting a couple of slices of bread, then spreading them liberally with mashed avocado, she returned to her room to eat, while watching the news. Hunger sated, she turned to her laptop. It was time she made a plan. A plan for the rest of her life. For if there was one thing the last few days had taught her, she never wanted to go back to being Abbey the party animal ever again.

CHAPTER 3

Present day...

In his dreams they appeared, the dead from the bomb at the Italian restaurant. Byrd shrunk away from them. He'd never seen anything like it. They were there, yet not there, flickering like an old black and white movie from a bygone era, preserved forever on celluloid film stock. He wanted to shout out to Jo, to warn her that she was surrounded by... By what? He had no bloody idea, but fear closed his throat in his dream, as it had in real life. He said nothing. He could do nothing. He was mute and frozen like a statue in a stately home garden. They were facing the man who Byrd guessed must be Odin, the terrorist they were seeking, who was masquerading as the leader of a new political party. Citing violence and murder to wipe away those who displeased him.

He thought perhaps they'd disappear, these apparitions. He hoped they would. But it only got worse, became more frightening, for then they spoke, one by one.

Mateo, the maître d': 'You took my life, left my wife a widow and my children fatherless. I'll never forgive you for that.'

Tony, the chef: 'How dare you take my precious restaurant. I was happy there. I poured all my heart into those dishes. I'll never forgive you for that.'

Paul the commis chef: 'I had my whole life before me. Years and years of happiness. My parents will never recover from their loss. I'll never forgive you for that.'

Nick, the pot wash: 'I had nothing. Then Tony believed in me and gave me a job. After years of being homeless on the streets, he held out the hand of friendship. Then you killed us and took away my future. I'll never forgive you for that.'

Byrd was shivering and shaking now. He was in the grip of his terror, losing his mind, but unable to break away from his nightmare.

Truelove the dodgy MP spat at Odin: 'I thought I was bad, but you are pure evil. I did what I did for money, but I never killed anyone. I'll never forgive you for all the lives you've taken.'

Truelove's wife: 'What did I ever do to you? I didn't know about my husband's dodgy dealings. But he didn't need to die for them and neither did I, nor my unborn child. I'll never forgive you for that.'

Then the remaining dead spoke all at once; John Jenkins, Harold Smith, Stephen McGrath, Lord Holland, Judge Chambers, Mr and Mrs Prendergast.

Finally, Alex Crooks' spirit left his body and joined them. 'I loved you and you took my love and threw it away like it was a piece of rubbish. I meant nothing to you. I'll never forgive you for that.'

They were all facing the terrorist, Odin. As they each confronted him with his evil and refused to pardon him *for his sins against them, they raised their hands. Byrd could see and feel the power flowing from them. A low hum began. Electrical energy surged through the warehouse. And it was all focused upon Odin. Their combined power took him to his knees. Odin raised his head and screamed out his anger and hatred of them. But it wasn't enough.*

With a clap of thunder, he splintered, the broken, jagged pieces of him suspended in the air for a moment. In one, Byrd saw his face, surprise and agony written across it, in another his slashed and burned torso, then one with arms and legs broken and bleeding. For one blinding moment they fused back together before finally turning into a single bolt of lightning that struck the ground and then burned out, never to be seen again. The God of War had fought his final battle and been found wanting.

One by one the dead faded away. The last one to go was Judith. Jo alone was left. She staggered, looking drained, but relieved it was all over.

Then Byrd found his voice.

'Jo?'

She turned.

'Jo, what the fuck just happened? What haven't you been telling me?'

Byrd clawed his way out of the nightmare and sat up in bed, gasping for air, his hair and body slick with sweat. The horror of what he'd seen and the outrage he felt towards Jo for keeping things from him, made him shake. Tremors rippled through his body. He'd taken the last couple of days off work, claiming incapacitation from a flu like bug. But that was a lie. Mind you, not as big a lie as the ones Jo had been telling him.

What the hell was going on in her life? He needed to ask her. But fear was paralysing him, and it was about time he put an end to it. He was a bloody detective for God's sake. He'd witnessed the depravity of men. Men like Odin. But he wasn't sure Odin had been a man, at all. What he actually was, Byrd had no idea. The fleeting thought of what he could be was too horrible to contemplate. And what was the deal with Judith? She'd died from the bomb in the restaurant. Hadn't she?

It was no good. He'd have to face his fears, for really it was fear of the unknown that was paralysing him. Maybe with a rational explanation he'd be able to come to terms with what he saw. Or at least what he thought he saw. But, of course, that meant he'd have to talk to Jo.

He grabbed his mobile phone from next to his bedside light and sent a text before he could change his mind: We need to meet.

Within minutes he had his reply: Yes, we do. Just tell me where and when. Jo x

CHAPTER 4

8 months ago...

Abbey had had an epiphany of sorts... she decided she must change her lifestyle, become clean and sober and find a way of supporting herself. She wanted a good future and long life and knew she had to change to achieve that. And she still remembered the nightmares she'd lived through in her dreams. She didn't think she'd ever forget them. If that's what drugs were doing to her, then she'd had enough of them.

She went for long walks, taking her neighbour's dog with her. The dog's natural enthusiasm for walks and life in general was infectious and Abbey began to get the germ of an idea of what she could do in terms of a job. It was so obvious, she wondered why she hadn't done it years ago. She would design and make clothes. Make use of that Art Degree she'd got several years ago and had pretty much ignored ever since. She'd sell her clothes on Etsy and eBay and maybe at the odd vintage market and promote them on Instagram and Facebook. After all, the one thing she knew about was social media, along with the rest of her generation, as they all spent much of their time online.

But she'd need a sewing machine and fabric. That could be difficult she reasoned. You can't exactly steal a sewing machine. Pop it in your pocket or an in an oversized handbag. Easily defeated she returned the dog to its owner and slouched off to the kitchen to make a coffee. If she could find any that was.

She was just about to open the kitchen door, when she saw something fluttering on the floor as though caught in a draught. It was a piece of paper. Hells bells, she thought, does no one pick up rubbish in this house? She stooped and grabbed the paper in her hand. She was astonished to find it wasn't a flyer or unwanted mail, but was a £20 note. Bloody hell. She looked around, but there was no one there. She had no idea who had dropped it. She shouted out to see if anyone was in, but there were no replies. She lived with 4 other housemates and there was normally someone around. She didn't want to take the money if it left someone else short. But maybe she could keep it and buy some food, or tobacco with it? She put it in her pocket, grabbed her coat from her room and went outside. Walking down the street she saw a couple of her housemates and she asked if they had dropped a £20 note. But they just shook their heads, said that Abbey had had a bit of luck and she should keep it. They would. Abbey kept fingering the note in her pocket. How strange the find was. But if no one was going to claim it, she may as well keep it. Nothing like that had ever happened to her before. Maybe her mates were right. What a piece of luck!

Mooching along the street Abbey stopped outside her favourite charity shop, toying with the idea of buying some clothes that she could regenerate or make into something better. Or some pieces of vintage clothing she could repair and sell on eBay. Looking through the window, her gaze fell on a polished wooden cabinet. It looked well-made but well worn. She went in and reaching into the window, she ran her hand across the wood. It felt warm, comforting, it felt like home, or rather a Hallmark view of home, certainly not her childhood home. Banishing thoughts of her troubled past, Abbey wondered where it could go in her room. She glanced at the ticket.

Oh goodness, it was a sewing machine. And the price? £20. It must be fate. It couldn't be anything else. She had to have it. Rushing over to the desk, she started gabbling at the volunteer, wanting to know if the machine worked. If she could have it. She must have it. She needed to have it.

'Oh yes it works, I tried it out this morning, see,' said the woman behind the counter, in a much calmer voice than Abbey's. The elderly assistant rummaged under the desk and pulled out a piece of cloth with machine stitching on it. 'This is what I did and as you can see it definitely works.'

'Could I have it please?' pleaded Abbey. 'I've just got £20. It's the last of my money.' Of course it was her only money, but she didn't want to admit to that.

'Sew, do you?' the woman asked as she plucked the ticket off the cabinet and wrote 'sold' on it. 'Sorry, what's your name? I need to put it on the ticket.'

'Oh hi, I'm Abbey and I'm trying to start a business, designing, and making, clothes. I studied that at Uni.'

'So I guess you're going to need material and threads?'

Oh God, Abbey hadn't thought of that. She

immediately deflated. Then realised how stupid that was. She had to stop being a pessimist. Turn into an optimist. A machine was a great first step. 'Yes, but I don't have any more money on me.'

'Hang on,' and the volunteer left the desk and disappeared into the back room.

All the time she was gone, Abbey was tapping her foot and trying to quell the worms of anxiety in her stomach. Was she sure she could do this? Really start a business and support herself? Or was she just dreaming. What was the saying? Pissing in the wind. That was it. She'd been told that all her life, why was it going to be any different this time?

Then the volunteer emerged, clutching an oversized plastic bag, chasing Abbey's bad vibes away. Looking closely, she appeared remarkably similar to the other volunteers who worked there, but Abbey hadn't seen her before. She must be new, Abbey reasoned. The woman's steel-grey hair looked like wire wool and didn't move. At all. It looked very stiff and Abbey wondered how she ever got a brush through it. She had on an old-fashioned dress and an overall or what used to be called a pinny, over it. Her grandmother had worn one. Abbey hadn't seen one since she'd died.

She caught Abbey looking at her clothes. 'Sorry about the pinny but I've been clearing out the stock room and it's very dusty back there. Anyway, look in here,' she said and opened the bag so Abbey could peek inside. 'We collected these, but never knew what to do with them.'

It was fabric. Lots of it. And thread. Bobbins of cotton of every hue and thickness. There was thick wool, traces of gauze and netting and strips of ribbon. It was better than Abbey could have ever imagined.

'Some of it is material that's been donated,' the

volunteer continued. 'The other stuff is clothes too damaged to sell but made of nice fabric. We just figured it would all find a good home eventually and it looks like that good home is you. Here, scribble down your address and the van can deliver your sewing machine later today. It's already going out, so one extra stop isn't going to matter to them.'

'But, but, I can't pay for delivery, I'll have to try and carry it, or get a mate to help me.'

'Nonsense, kindness costs nothing. Now off you go, take the bag with you and good luck. Maybe we'll see some of your designs on the telly one day. You never know!'

Abbey thanked the woman profusely and skipped out of the shop before the volunteer could change her mind.

Once at home and while waiting for the sewing machine and cabinet to be delivered, Abbey pulled out a box she had with all her university stuff in it and found the designs she'd sketched. She also found a new sketch pad, pencils, pens, a few samples she'd made up for her exams and the end of year fashion show. How could she have forgotten all this stuff? Her pride in her work rushed back as she recaptured the buzz of University, lost so long ago. She had obtained a First-Class degree and several enthusiastic endorsements of her work. The waste of her achievements weighed heavily on her shoulders and Abbey wondered what had happened to her? But, of course, she knew, deep down. The parties, the drugs, the alcohol, had all taken over, became more important than getting a job or building a business. Being an entrepreneur was hard. Being a party animal was easy.

Still, the endorsements were valid at the time and perhaps she could still use them in her advertising copy.

Her theme had not been so much vintage 1950's, more 1960's mod, although that was vintage now wasn't it? After all it was the 2020's and the 1960's was a lifetime ago. She remembered her interest in the era had been piqued after a visit to the Victoria and Albert museum in London. She needed to go back there. Checking the V&A website, it confirmed that admission was still free. She would go tomorrow, if she could borrow the train fare, or maybe try and dodge paying. She'd take her mobile phone with her to take pictures and her sketch pad to record ideas. Excitement fizzed in her blood. She might have lost the last 10 years to partying, but she was damned if she was going to waste the next 10.

CHAPTER 5

Present day...

Jo threw her mobile onto the bed as tears of relief filled her eyes. At last she'd heard from Byrd. He wanted to arrange to meet up. The past few days had been beyond surreal. She still couldn't make much sense of what had happened when she'd faced Odin and everyone who had died at his hand had begun to appear. No one at the station, apart from her and Byrd, knew what had happened at the warehouse that night. Jo just called it a meeting with Odin, who never showed up and unfortunately Alex Crook had suffered a suspected heart attack at the scene, probably brought on by the stress of going undercover in the British Nordic League. They'd called the emergency services, but he was dead by the time they got there.

But the worst thing in all the debacle? She could lose Byrd. At work he'd been tight lipped, only speaking to her when absolutely necessary and then he'd disappeared. Said he wasn't well. Hadn't been answering the telephone, nor his door. As the hours and days had gone by without a word or sign from him as to how he felt, Jo had become morose and defeated. She'd fought the battle with Odin and won, but now she had another battle to face. The battle to get Byrd to understand who, and what, she was. Hopefully that would be the last thing she'd have to face out of the whole disaster. Once Byrd was once more with her, life could return to normal. At least Jo's normal.

She fell back and rested on the pillows. Light was beginning to poke fingers from behind the curtains and the birds were signalling the start of a new day. With a bit of luck, a better day. She had dozed off again when her phone pinged with a message and woke her up.

Grabbing her phone, she read the text from Byrd: Mid-day. Your place.

Checking her watch, Jo realised she needed to hurry and get ready and then tidy up the flat. Not forgetting to go and buy the Sunday papers and some food. Perhaps Byrd would stay for brunch?

Feeling better after a shower, Jo wrapped herself in a towel and wiped away the condensation on the bathroom mirror.

There was Judith. Standing just behind Jo's shoulder. Jo stilled, hardly believing her eyes. Judith should be at peace now, not appearing to her. She turned around and... nothing. There was no one there.

Jo shrugged and turned back to the sink. It was more than likely that she was feeling lonely and missing her friend. What with all this business with Byrd. But that wouldn't explain the unsettling feeling she was experiencing. A crawling of her skin. Cold breath caressing the back of her neck. She straightened up and though afraid, she glanced in the mirror once more. To see Judith peeking over her shoulder. Looking around, Jo found the bathroom was still empty. Turning back to the mirror, there was Judith.

It seemed Judith wasn't resting in peace after all. She must want something. To dispel the panic building inside her, Jo decided it was best just to have a conversation with Judith, no matter how weird it may seem. For what could happen? What was there to be frightened of? It was only her friend, after all.

'Hey, Judith.'

Judith smiled. So she'd heard Jo. Or perhaps Jo was hallucinating. Or still asleep and dreaming. There was that.

But then Judith spoke. 'You're wondering what I'm doing here.'

Jo wasn't sure whether to be relieved or terrified. She picked relieved and after a deep breath said, 'You could say that. I thought this ghostly apparition thing was done and dusted. You know, since Odin. It should be all over by now.'

'Not quite.' Judith smiled. 'It seems I'm going to be around for a while longer yet.'

'But why? What the hell is going on?' Jo was beginning to lose the battle with containing her emotions, her fear began to manifest itself in anger. She wasn't happy about this. Not at all.

'It seems that defeating evil is to be your destiny and mine is to help you and be your contact in the spirit world.'

'Sod my destiny! Why do I need you? We face evil every day in the killers we chase. We do a good job. A worthwhile job.' Jo closed her eyes. Perhaps Judith would go away if Jo wasn't looking at her. She gripped the side of the sink, the cool porcelain reassuringly solid.

'You'll need me for guidance and help in future cases.'

So much for that theory, Judith was still there. Defeated, Jo opened her eyes. 'But I investigate murders.'

'Yes, but from now on you'll be faced with murders that involve the supernatural.'

Jo thought of Anubis and Odin and shuddered. She didn't want to go there again. Face creatures like them. She went weak at the thought and her voice shook as she said, 'But what if I don't want to? It isn't fair!' She could hear the plaintive tones in her voice. It was as though she were 10 years old, not 30. A child again, not a seasoned detective.

'I'm afraid you don't have much choice in the matter, Jo, and neither do I. We have been specially chosen. So, will you join me willingly?'

But Jo wasn't having any of it. She ignored Judith, dropped her towel on the floor and ran from the bathroom, slamming the door behind her. She took refuge in her bedroom, where there weren't any mirrors. Shaking the image of Judith in the glass from her mind, she concentrated on getting ready to meet Byrd. She was furious. How dare they invade her home! They, Judith, whoever they were. Taking liberties. She must have some say in the matter. Surely?

Was this the price she had to pay for her recovery? If she'd known that at the time would she have wanted to live, or to die? Then she thought of her family, her father in particular. And then Byrd. If she'd had died after the riding accident, they would never have met. What was that quotation: It is better to have loved and lost, than never to have loved at all? Yeah, there was that. Okay so she wouldn't have wanted to die. But that didn't make this emotional blackmail stuff right. It was all wrong. But she was stuck in the middle, trying to walk the tightrope between her normal life and her job, and her supernatural life and the creatures she came up against. There was a lot of evil out there in the world and she'd only seen a small amount of it. Only scratched the surface. She knew there was only one answer that she could give to Judith's question and with resignation in every step, Jo walked back to the bathroom to give Judith her decision.

CHAPTER 6

Jo had made a lunch of cheeses, paté, freshly baked baguettes, and red wine. Very French. It was the best she could come up with at short notice. Her cookery skills were negligible. She'd texted her father to let him know that Byrd was coming to see her and that she wouldn't make the short journey from her flat above the garage to the main house for lunch with the family. He'd understand. He knew what Byrd meant to her.

Her doorbell rang. Oh God he's here, she thought and looked down at her hands, which were shaking. She needed a glass of that rather nice Merlot breathing on the kitchen table.

She lifted the handset of the intercom, but found she couldn't speak, so she just pressed the door lock to let Byrd in.

Within moments, he was there. There was a minute of social awkwardness as neither knew whether to kiss or not. Jo took a step back from him and said, 'Good to see you, Byrd.'

He nodded, 'And you, ma'am.'

Jo's eyes blazed, but then realised he was smiling at her, maybe trying to break the ice by teasing her with the hated greeting for a senior officer. She thumped him on the arm good naturedly and they both smiled.

'A drink?' Jo indicated the table.

'Please,' and Byrd poured them a glass each. 'Nice spread,' he offered, indicating the table.

'Just a little something I threw together.'

'With the help of Messrs Marks and Spencer?'

Jo smiled. 'Of course. They've never let me down yet. Shall we sit?'

Sitting at the table was better than being awkwardly thrown together on her small settee. And anyway, passing the bread, butter and cheese gave her hands something to do. The only problem was that Jo wasn't sure if she could get food past the blockage in her throat.

'Byrd,' she began. 'It's about time I told you everything about me.'

He nodded his agreement. 'That would be a good idea. A good place to start.'

Jo took a gulp of the water she'd placed on the table as well as the wine. 'It all began with an accident.'

'The riding accident?'

'Yes, that one,' and Jo began haltingly to tell him about her recovery and how the kick to her head from the horse had changed her.

As she spoke, Byrd began to nibble on the food and he topped up their wine glasses. It appeared he was relaxing, thank goodness.

'So during the Anubis investigation and the Odin one,' Byrd said, 'you were able to touch the dead and see what had happened to them.'

'Yes, as far as the Anubis case went. But during the Odin one, I began to see what was happening to the living as well.'

'Bloody hell, that must have been pretty hairy.'

Jo smiled. Encouraged by Byrd's seeming acceptance of her gift, she talked to him about Judith and her role in past investigations and quite possibly future ones. By the time she'd finished, they'd eaten and drunk their fill.

'Coffee?' she asked.

'Good idea.'

Jo went into the kitchen and messed about with the coffee pot, ground coffee and water. Her hands had started shaking again. She'd not had much of a reaction out of Byrd so far and couldn't imagine what was going to happen next.

Then Byrd entered the kitchen. She froze. Not knowing what to do, she stayed facing the wall. He moved towards her. She could smell his aftershave and it made her go weak at the knees. Then he was standing behind her, his arms snaking around her waist. She leaned back against him as he lifted her hair and began to kiss her neck. Tingles ran up and down her spine. Then he turned her to face him...

Sometime later, wrapped in his arms and tangled in the sheets on her bed, she asked, 'Are you OK, Byrd. You know, with all of this?'

'Honestly?'

Jo thought that an odd thing to say, she leaned her head backwards so she could see his face. 'Of course.' But uncertainty was gnawing away at her. She suddenly didn't feel so sure of Byrd anymore. Again.

He looked down at her. 'I'm not sure how I feel about all this. I... I have very strong feelings for you, you know that, Jo. But... Oh I don't know. I appreciate your honesty, but I think I need a while to process it. You know?'

Jo did. She'd had enough trouble coming to terms with it herself, so she had to give Byrd time to come to his own decision. But the disappointment she felt made her stomach drop, as though she'd been in a lift going too fast towards the ground floor. It seemed that in the cold light of day, Byrd still wasn't sure about her gift. Or curse. Yes it was absolutely becoming a curse. If she lost Byrd because of it, she wouldn't know what to do.

He kissed her, to maybe try and take some of the sting out of his words? But to Jo it felt more like a goodbye.

CHAPTER 7

6 months ago...

Abbey stretched awake. Looking around her room, in the growing morning light, she could see her sewing corner neat and tidy, ready for the day's work. Hanging from a rail were clothes waiting to be posted to customers. Her laptop was open at the press release she was going to send out to try and drum up interest from bloggers and the like. Life over the past three months had been good. At long last her life was stable. She knew that three months wasn't a long time for a fledgling business. But it was the longest period of being clean and sober that Abbey had managed in years. Her local job centre had put her forward for the self-employed business development scheme, which gave her extra money for sourcing clothes and materials. And the regular monthly Universal Credit payment meant she could pay her rent and feed herself. Just.

Yes, life was... her thought was cut short as she inexplicably felt nauseous. Clasping her hand over her mouth she sprang from the bed and dashed to the toilet where she was sick. Returning on shaking legs, she got back into bed and sipped water, before rushing back to the toilet and bringing it all back up again. Shaking and shivery Abbey wondered if she had a virus and climbed back into bed. If she was honest with herself this wasn't the first time it had happened. She'd just put it down to the withdrawal her body must be going through from the years of drug and alcohol abuse. But maybe it was something else. Something more.

By the third day of similar behaviour, Abbey had, with growing horror, bought a pregnancy test. She tried to remember when she'd last had a period, but couldn't. Mind you, that wasn't unusual. Her hit and miss lifestyle when it came to food and illegal substances meant that her cycle wasn't always as regular as it should be. She read the instruction leaflet for the test with shaking hands, and a feeling of dread.

After placing the stick under a stream of urine, she continued to sit on the toilet while she waited for the blue line.

And then there it was. Irrefutable evidence. She was pregnant.

Oh dear God. What would she do? Who could she turn to? Who would support her during this… this disaster?

Her parents had finally washed their hands of her last year. She knew she'd repeatedly hurt and upset them with her irresponsible behaviour, rashness with money, and an angry and volatile personality. When she saw them, she was mostly on a come down from a particularly high dose of illegal substance. Therefore, they didn't trust her anymore and who could blame them really? She'd been a bad person, but that wasn't her any longer. But would they believe her? Probably not. Her only friends were other drug users and party animals, so they would be of no help at all.

Deciding that fresh air might help both her deliberations and her nausea, she dressed quickly and went out into the early morning sunshine. Walking past the cathedral she decided to have a look around. Even though she lived in Chichester, she couldn't remember ever going inside. There was a sign saying that entry was free, but donations would be appreciated.

Surprised the building was open so early, a soaring melody from the organ drew her inside and she wandered around listening to the expert playing and wondered if someone was practicing. Dismayed when the instrument fell silent, she saw a man leave the organ loft and climb down. As he emerged into the body of the cathedral, she told him how much she'd enjoyed his playing. He was probably about the same age as her and dressed in clerical garb. They introduced themselves and she found out his name was Osian Price and that he was one of the clergy attached to the cathedral. He invited her to walk around the interior with him, but she was beginning to feel unwell. She broke out into a sweat and her stomach clenched, the pain making her double over. Gasping for air, she mumbled something to Osian and fled. She didn't know why but she had to get out of the cathedral. Fast. There was something dreadfully wrong with either her or the building. She didn't know which and to be honest didn't care. She ran like she was pursued by the hounds of hell. Once she broke out into the gardens and the sunlight, she started to feel better. Her breathing slowed; her pulse rate returned to normal.

Unsure as to what had just happened, Abbey thought that perhaps she'd picked up a bug. Her stomach was still sore, as though she'd been kicked in it and she once again felt sick. Rushing to a rubbish bin, she vomited into it, holding on with shaking hands. Once the wave of sickness was over, Abbey straightened and wiped her mouth with a tissue. Her stomach clenched again. She had to get home before she made a complete fool of herself.

With a lingering backward look at the cathedral and if she was honest, Osian, Abbey turned away and ran for home, not noticing the extra gargoyle sat atop the cathedral wall. Watching.

CHAPTER 8

Present day...

It was time for Jo's meeting with the new boss. Since Alex Crooks died, the force had been casting around for a new Detective Chief Inspector. Jo had imagined it would be an internal appointment but was as surprised as everyone else when it was announced that an experienced DCI was joining them from Manchester. By all accounts Harry Sykes was a dour Yorkshire man who had moved down south to get away from the rain! He was fed up with the cold climate of the North and appreciated being near to the sea. As far as anyone knew he'd moved here on his own. But there were no details on his marital status. Jo had heard that someone was starting a 'book' on how long he'd last, but she'd passed on the opportunity of putting £5 on the odds-on favourite of just six months.

As far as Jo was aware, Sykes knew nothing of any strange circumstances surrounding Jo's last two cases and she wanted to keep it that way. Everyone thought that Alex had had a heart attack at the scene of the confrontation with Odin. Crooks died, Odin must have flown the coop as he'd not turned up for the meeting and hadn't been seen since, and life in Chichester had returned to some semblance of normal.

'Ah, Jo, good to meet you.' DCI Harry Sykes welcomed Jo into his office. The one that used to belong to Alex Crook. It held many memories for Jo and she was surprised to see that Sykes hadn't made any changes. In fact some of Alex's things were still there, pictures on the walls, paper tray on the desk and, of course, Alex's chair. Maybe no one had wanted them. After all he had been divorced, so it was doubtful his ex-wife had wanted anything personal from it. That was a sad thought, that there was no one in Alex's life who cared enough. She hoped that wouldn't happen to her. She considered the thought that maybe many lonely years stretched in front of her. But that was too horrible to contemplate. Shaking that depressing view of life off her shoulders, she brought herself back to the here and now.

Jo managed a small smile at Sykes' greeting and shook his hand. 'Good to meet you too, Sir.'

'Please, have a seat.'

Jo sat opposite Sykes as he returned to his chair. She was wearing her usual trouser-suit and a crisp white blouse. She'd put on heels, that she'd take off as soon as she reached her office. Her short black pixie hairstyle had recently been trimmed and she was wearing subtle make up and a swipe of lip gloss.

'You and your team have been through the mill lately, I hear.'

'Yes, we've had a particularly difficult case. What with the bombing and... everything.'

'But this,' Sykes looked at his notes, 'Odin character hasn't been heard from since the confrontation in the warehouse.'

'No, Sir,' Jo struggled to keep her face blank at the mention of Odin. 'And as he's disappeared, so the party has just about disappeared as well, the British Nordic League, that is. I don't think we'll hear much more from them.'

'Well, let's hope not. Before we move on, just remind me again why and how Odin managed to get away?'

'It was because Alex collapsed, at least that's our guess. Our focus was firmly on the DCI. We tried to revive him, but unfortunately, he died at the scene. We never saw Odin, so to be honest, Sir, we don't know if he turned up or not.'

'Remind me, the 'we' was you and DS Byrd?'

'That's correct, Sir.'

'Um, well, not exactly protocol was it? Going in without back-up?'

Jo held her breath, wondering what was coming next. This meeting was already far more difficult that she'd hoped. She struggled to keep her hands still in her lap and her feet flat on the floor.

Sykes looked at her for a few seconds, then appeared to have come to a decision, as he said, 'But nevertheless understandable, given Alex Crooks' state of mind at the time, by all accounts.'

Jo exhaled. 'Thank you, Sir,' she managed to mumble, with relief. Unbidden was a thought that perhaps he might just be tricking her into thinking all was well, when it wasn't and that she'd be under investigation before she could say 'supernatural'.

As the conversation moved onto safer ground, Jo looked at Sykes more closely. His face reflected what he was, a dour Yorkshire man. It was all lines and angles and with no spare flesh. He didn't seem much given to humour, nor light-hearted conversation. She could smell cigarette smoke on his clothes. He wore a non-descript suit, coloured shirt and dark tie. Nothing that stood out. He was tall, over 6ft, thin and rangy and looked like the sort of bloke who faded into the background. But perhaps that was a ploy. You didn't get to the rank of DCI by being invisible.

They briefly talked about Jo's open cases and then he said, 'It seems that my previous incumbent, Alex Crook, had you pencilled in for the nasty, major crimes cases. Is that right?'

'Yes, Sir, we are the team for murder cases and the like in Chichester and sometimes the wider area.'

'And you want that to stay?'

Jo was beginning to sense that she was on shaky ground again. 'Oh, very much, Sir,' she tried to sound as positive as possible. 'The team are pretty tight knit and used to working together.'

'And that team is?'

'DS Eddie Byrd, DC Jill Sandy, DC Ken Guest, and DS Sasha Gold providing computer and office management support. Plus we also work with Bill Burke from forensics and Jeremy Grogan, the pathologist.'

'And DS Gold is happy being office bound?'

'Very, she works well on her own, is able to prioritise and provide answers to most questions and problems thrown at her.'

'Very well,' Sykes nodded his agreement. 'Let's keep things that way then and we'll review it again once you've finished your next case.'

Jo could breathe again and managed, 'Are there any new cases you want us on, Sir?'

'No, not as yet. Wrap up the Odin case and let's see what comes up.'

Jo took that as a dismissal and stood. 'Thank you, Sir,' she said and left.

Bloody hell, she was glad to get out of the office. She'd felt like the walls were closing in on her. But Sykes hadn't given anything away. Hadn't shown her anything of his personality (if he had one, she thought rebelliously). She didn't know what to make of him. She'd just have to wait until they got an active investigation, he'd no doubt show his true colours then. She made a mental note to ask her dad about Sykes. He'd know any gossip about the DCI for sure.

CHAPTER 9

Jill sat in Chichester cathedral listening to the choir. The clear notes, sung to perfection lightened her heart and soul. Since joining Major Crimes, Jill had found it hard to relax in her time off, at evenings and weekends. At least the time off she had once an investigation had concluded. Until then it was pretty much 24/7 for all the team members.

Feeling exhausted and drained she'd wondered how to best counteract that. To find an interest that she could dip in and out of as time permitted. She'd tried Pilates (too exerting), Yoga (too boring), Sailing (too wet), long walks (lonely without a dog). Passing the Cathedral one day she'd come across an advert for a free lunchtime recital, and from then on, she was hooked.

Having a religious background (which she kept quiet and who wouldn't?) she was familiar with the services, but it wasn't until she went to choral evensong at the Cathedral that she truly appreciated the choir and particularly the choristers. She always thought she'd had enough of church, as she'd grown up with a cleric for a father. She'd had enough of the lack of money, the sense of service (always being at someone's beck and call) and cold draughty houses that don't belong to you.

But it seemed faith hadn't had enough of her. Her interest re-kindled, she began to attend services regularly and it was there that she'd met Osian Price. At first it was nothing more than a welcome friendship. She didn't really know anyone in Chichester apart from members of the force. As her interest in the cathedral grew, she signed up to be a volunteer, as the organisers were happy to slot her in at short notice when she had some free time. She became interested in Osian's role in the Cathedral and likewise he became interested in her working life.

They decided, over copious cups of coffee and the occasional meal out, that they both served. Jill, the public in her role as a detective constable and Osian, serving God in the cathedral. He had no interest in being a parish priest and she had no interest in leaving the force. They began, slowly, to realise that their relationship might, just, flourish under the umbrella of service.

Once Evensong finished, she held back and so she managed a few snatched minutes with Osian before he rushed to the training course he was giving for volunteers. Unbeknown to her, they were about to be thrown together, when their jobs would fuse into one. And they would have to make the ultimate decision. Would they have enough faith in order to prevail?

CHAPTER 10

3 months ago...

Abbey walked around the Cathedral gardens. The weather was warm, the birds were singing, tourists were flocking into the cathedral itself. She had on a comfortable maternity dress, blue with white polka dots. Her hair was scraped back in a ponytail and she had flat sandals on her feet. She was as comfortable as she could be. Abbey never went inside the Cathedral anymore, not since that awful day when she'd been so sick and made a complete and utter fool of herself. Several times she'd got to the door but had had to turn away. It was as though she were having a panic attack. Her breathing went shallow, she started to shake, her head spun, and she could barely see. She'd resorted to getting out of the way of people and leaning against the cathedral wall, looking outward, unable to go in.

Occasionally she saw Osian, which was always a plus. Cause for a definite lightening of her mood. But there could never be anything between them. She wasn't at all religious and if she was, she supposed she was a Catholic. Which would be a bit awkward as Chichester Cathedral was a protestant church.

The other reason though, was that she could sense a barrier between them. Let's face it she was about to become and unmarried mother. She didn't even know who the child's father was. She knew she couldn't get too close to him, that way led pain and unhappiness and that wasn't what she wanted for herself and her baby.

She greedily drank the bottle of water she'd brought with her, before attempting the walk home. The baby wasn't due for another three months and to be honest she couldn't wait. Osian told her that if she had trouble affording clothes and other necessities for the baby, the church were happy to help. She'd thanked him and said that the business was doing well, so she should be okay. He told her to keep his offer in mind. There was nothing wrong with accepting a helping hand.

Maybe that was the barrier between them. She was so fiercely independent now, she didn't want anything from anybody. This was her fight, hers alone and she was determined not to be found wanting. She didn't need any distractions. Her fledgling business was all consuming, just as it should be.

When she arrived home, Abbey sat down with a huff. She hardly recognised herself anymore. Her ankles were swollen, her tummy was swollen, her back ached, her legs ached. And she felt like a sack of bloody potatoes.

She looked in the mirror, posing this way and that. The body was bloody awful but her face, maybe not. She did seem to be blooming. She ticked off the imaginary list; hair good, nails good, the new regime and lifestyle was definitely working. Perhaps she should take some selfies and share an update with her followers on

Facebook and Instagram. Normally she posted about her clothes, but maybe they'd like a more personal one.

Everything was going well. Perhaps it was too good to be true? That was always her mantra. Something could go wrong. Would go wrong. Deep down she was a pessimist, not an optimist. She had no problems striving, just problems accepting her good fortune.

She looked over her order book. That confirmed she had plenty to keep her busy. Business was booming. She had enough orders for her to work steadily, keeping to deadlines and yet producing an excellent product at a value for money price.

Then the baby kicked. It was as though he wanted out. Of course he did. She wanted him out too. But there was that worry again. How would she manage the business with a new baby? The first two or three months would be horrendous. There would be no sleep, there could be problems with breast feeding and the baby would take all her time, energy, and focus. What would happen to the business then? She had to implement a work around. A plan to keep the business going. Together with keeping herself sane.

The problem was that she had no idea how to achieve it.

CHAPTER 11

Present day...

Byrd felt like the world had been plunged into an ice age. He was so very cold. All the way to his soul. The weather was cold. He was cold. His emotions were cold. He could feel the vestiges of his fear, anger, and revulsion he'd felt as he had witnessed the strange events in the warehouse. Those 'spirits' he supposed they were. And Jo at their head. Their leader. Nothing about that time made any sense to him.

Jo had told him all about herself and about the gift she had. At the time, when they were full of food and wine and in the afterglow of sex, it seemed perfectly plausible. Jo was still Jo, she was just... plus, he supposed. She was more than the Jo he knew, she had a gift, or curse. But as time went on, Byrd was beginning to feel it was a curse. Yes, a curse. It was something he just couldn't deal with.

As a result he'd starting avoiding her at work. Sometimes he caught sight of her sadness at what might have been. It was in her eyes. Her pain was almost the undoing of him, but he hardened his heart against her. Felt that life would be better without her.

But that decision had taken him into the coldness of a life without Jo in it.

He awoke with a start.

The bed clothes were in a heap by his feet. He was shivering. That must have been why he was cold. Why the plunging temperature had invaded his dream, then woken him up. He pulled the duvet back over him and burrowed down into its warmth. He was immediately asleep again.

He luxuriated in the heat. The sun was shining. He wasn't alone. Jo was with him. She was smiling. They were sitting outside in the park, having a picnic. He basked in the warmth of the weather and the company.

Jo laughed at something he'd said, and he lent forward and kissed her. She kissed him back with an urgency that matched his own. Both agreeing to leave, they piled their stuff into the car and raced back to his flat. Jo had transformed his dull, dank space into a small, but welcoming apartment. Just her mere presence had done most of it. They ran through the door and collapsed on the bed, resuming their earlier intimacy.

He drifted off into a post coital, dreamless sleep.

But it was Judith who woke him, not Jo. Judith? He cast around for her but couldn't find her. He noticed he was still in bed. Why was she in his flat? Where had she gone? 'Judith?' he asked.

'Hey, Byrd,' she said, making Byrd jump. She had appeared in the mirror opposite his bed. 'So what do you think of my dream?'

'Sorry?'

This was a surreal conversation. Judith was dead. Why

could he see her in the mirror? How was that even possible? What the hell was going on? Byrd began to shiver. Only this time, it was from fear.

'Which scenario do you prefer, Byrd?'

'Eh?'

'Without Jo. Or with Jo. A life of coldness, or a life of sunshine?'

He didn't need to think about the answer to that question. 'A life of sunshine, obviously,' he chose.

'So are you happy to accept her for what she is? Who she is? Are you going to celebrate her gift, or hate her for it? The choice is yours. Make sure it's the right one.'

Byrd awoke, sweat pouring from him. Did Judith just appear to him in a dream? Whatever had just happened had frightened him. Made him feel like he'd just had a visit from Marley's ghost. He could hear chains clanking in the distance as the apparition walked away. The way Judith had talked, it was an easy decision to make about his future. He didn't want a life without Jo. He wanted the sunshine. The happiness. He wanted her. So he'd just have to accept her, warts and all. Wouldn't he?

But was it necessary to frighten him into a decision? Really? Who would do such a thing?

He felt a breath on the back of his neck and a shiver down his spine. He looked at his arms and the hairs there were all standing on end.

'It's okay, Judith, I'll make my peace with Jo.'

Then he wondered what the hell he was doing talking to an empty room. But it wasn't empty was it? He could feel a change in the air, in the atmosphere, as though he wasn't the only one in the flat. He got out of bed and dressed just in his boxers, walked to the bedroom door. He held his breath. Who was there? He couldn't see any light under the door, but he eased it open just the same.

His bedroom was at the end of a corridor that ran along the length of the flat. He had to walk along it to get to the lounge, so that's what he did. He found himself inching along the wall, back and hands touching the plaster, anchoring him to the here and now. His emotions were skittering all over the place and he shivered. It was becoming harder and harder to put one foot in front of the other as the dread mounted in him and flowed through his veins like molten lead.

He turned right at the end of the hallway into the lounge. As he did, he caught sight of Judith, just out of the corner of his eye, reflected in the mirror over the fireplace. In an instant she was gone and he thought she'd fled into the hall and out through the front door. But that wasn't possible. The front door was shut and locked. Had she walked through it? His legs buckled and he hit the floor.

Staying where he sat with his back to the wall, he tried to examine himself. Could he feel his limbs, fingers and toes? Yes. Could he straighten his legs? Yes. Could he see and hear okay? Yes.

Then what the hell had he just seen. It must have been a figment of his imagination. Because he'd been dreaming of Judith. Nothing more than that. His eyes and brain playing tricks on him. Taking deep breaths, he noticed it was 6.30 am. There was no need to go back to bed where he'd just play what had happened over and over in his mind. He'd turn on the TV for company and make a pot of strong coffee. That should banish all thoughts of ghosts and visitations. But his legs still trembled, and his hands shook as he stood and walked to the kitchen.

CHAPTER 12

3 months ago...

The following day Abbey pushed through the door of her favourite charity shop and saw that Edith, who helped her buy the sewing machine all those months ago, was behind the counter. Pleased to see a friendly face, Abbey told Edith that she desperately needed help, but didn't have anyone to turn to. She was on the hunt for a talented seamstress, but had had no luck finding anyone so far, at least no one who would work for the little money Abbey was able to pay. Did Edith know of anyone?

'What sort of thing would you want someone to do?' Edith asked and Abbey noticed the woman's eyes seemed to be dancing with interest.

'Well it could be either altering clothes or making new ones from scratch. Just following my designs really. I would do all the creative work while the baby is little, if someone else could then take over and produce the clothes.'

All the while Edith's smile had been getting wider. 'I could help you,' she offered.

'Really?' Jo said looking at Edith, who to her looked about a 100 years old.

'Oh yes, I'd be glad to. I've always made my own clothes. Mother was a seamstress and I followed her into the profession. I only volunteer at the shop because I'm retired, and it gives me something to do. But I'd be glad to help. I can pop backwards and forward to you and work on the garments at home.'

Abbey was still doubtful. 'I can't ask that of you, Edith. You should be enjoying your retirement, not slaving away over a hot sewing machine!'

Edith laughed. 'I'm not as old as I look and I'm pretty robust you know. If it makes you feel better, I'll stop volunteering in the shop, so I'm not overreaching myself. Go on, Abbey, help me feel wanted and useful again. It's so exciting to see you doing so well and I'd love to be a part of that.'

Put like that how could Abbey refuse? The suggestion seemed ideal. But there was still a small nagging doubt that perhaps Edith's offer was too good to be true. Aware that Edith was still looking at her, waiting for her answer, and frankly as she had no other options, Abbey nodded. 'Thank you, Edith. It sounds ideal. Shall we have a coffee to celebrate?'

Edith clasped her hands together and clapped her fingers. 'Oh, goody, that's perfect. Thank you so much, Abbey. I won't let you down I promise. Now, just let me get my coat, it's time for my break anyway, but this is my treat, my way of saying thank you.'

As Edith toddled off to the private area where the donations were sorted and priced, Abbey hoped to God she'd made the right choice. She didn't want to be responsible for Edith as well as the baby, should things go pear shaped. There was that glass half full thing again, Abbey admonished herself. Nothing was going to go wrong she hoped, rubbing her stomach, as she felt the baby kick.

Edith hurried into the back of the shop, eager to get her things, before Abbey changed her mind. So much was riding on this birth, she knew, and she'd done everything she could so far to encourage Abbey to keep the baby. Edith had played her part well and was sure the Watcher would reward her handsomely for it. Although perhaps next time she could be a beautiful young woman, instead of the old crone he'd insisted she become this time. Well, perhaps old crone was a bit harsh, she decided. She felt she looked more like a fairy godmother in a Disney movie, or at least that's how she needed to come across to Abbey. Intent on becoming the parent that the poor girl had lost, she'd ensured Abbey had everything she needed to make a success of her new business, enabling her to build a solid future for her and the baby.

As she emerged from behind the curtain, her eyes narrowed as she watched Abbey, who was standing by the door. Yes, with Edith's help and the backing of a guardian angel (albeit a fallen one Edith thought, one side of her mouth rising in an ironic smile), what could possibly go wrong?

With Edith's help Abbey would keep the money coming in and she'd have time to look after the baby, both objectives that would keep the Watcher happy. It was important to keep the baby with the mother for as long as possible. But no more than absolutely necessary, at least before some of the changes in its development were noticed. And then once the time was right, Edith would take the baby and disappear. No one would ever find the child, because no one would ever find Edith. She wouldn't be found as she wouldn't exist anymore. She'd already have changed form and become someone else. And even if the unthinkable should happen and the baby found and re-united with Abbey, well then Edith (or rather her new persona) would appear in Abbey's life and befriend her.

As usual, the Watcher had thought of everything.

Waiting for Edith, Abbey mooched around the shop fingering fabrics, checking out styles, smiling and nodding to other customers. She'd always loved this shop, especially since meeting Edith. It was one of those places where she felt welcome, accepted, and not judged.

Wandering towards the door, she felt a cold breath on the back of her neck. Whirling around, expecting to see another browser, there was no one there, only Edith at the opening to the back room of the shop. Perhaps it was a draft from the shop door, so she turned back to the door. But no, it was firmly closed. Frowning, she shivered and a saying her grandmother was fond of crossed her mind: someone just walked over my grave.

CHAPTER 13

Present day...

It wasn't just Byrd having a restless night, Jo was also. She could not settle. She dozed off, then woke again. Read a bit, fell asleep, then woke again. And the dreams! She kept reliving the explosion in the Italian restaurant. Then the taking down of Odin. It was like the worst cases of PTSD, but she was asleep. Nightmares on a loop that she couldn't shake free from.

Everywhere she turned in her dream world, Judith was there.

And she was there when Jo woke and went to the bathroom.

Once more, Jo saw Judith in the bathroom mirror. But this time, Jo refused to be frightened. In fact, she was beginning to be resigned to seeing Judith every time she looked in the mirror. Not your normal feature of an apartment. They'd have a hard time explaining that to an estate agent should they ever try and sell the house. Vacant possession, that would be a laugh. No humans, just a resident ghost.

Grabbing hold of the sink, she said, 'Okay, let's have it. What do you want, Judith?'

'Hey, how are you?'

'Oh, you know...' Jo's eyes watered at the thought of what her life had become without Byrd. Cold. Empty. Full of grey clouds. But still, she pulled herself together, life must go on.

'Yes, I know,' Judith said.

Her friend's expression of tenderness was almost the undoing of Jo. She sniffed loudly and pulled some toilet paper off the roll, blowing her nose and then throwing the tissue into the toilet.

'I thought an explanation of how things are evolving, might help you,' continued Judith. 'It appears that it was my fate to die that terrible night of the bomb. But it's not all bad, because I've becomes your spirit guide and I'm good with that.'

'You are? But what does 'my spirit guide' even mean?' Jo couldn't get her head around these developments. It had all started with a gift enabling her to 'read' objects, but it was now spiralling out of her control. Taking down evil spirits and now needing a spirit guide! Jo wished this was all a dream and she could go back to bed and wake up again to a life without ghostly figures in it.

'Spirit guides are beings that come to humans to assist them in their life's journey. They are spirits of those who were once human and have attained a higher level of spiritual mastery. They retain an awareness of human beings living on Earth and volunteer to help individuals in all facets of life.'

'Volunteer?'

Judith smiled. 'Alright, not volunteer exactly, but that's neither here nor there. In moments of sorrow and *desperation, your spirit guide can lightly touch you. If you are in danger of getting hurt, you may feel a push or tug.'*

'Or even see an apparition in a mirror?'

'Exactly. Look, you know what we can achieve together. We defeated Odin, didn't we?'

'Well, yes, not that I can talk to anyone about it. Only my dad and Byrd. But I don't want to talk about Byrd. He's not in my life anymore. We tried, but it didn't work out. We're just colleagues.'

'Well, things might be looking up there.'

'What? Look, Judith, don't give me false hope. I couldn't bear it.'

'No false hope, Jo, I promise. Anyway, back to spirit guides. You can always talk to Keith Thomas about the concept.'

'Or Google it.'

Judith smiled. 'Or Google it,' she agreed. 'Anyway, there's something happening, but I'm not sure what. There are bad vibes going round. Something is stirring, something evil and powerful. Keep a look out, Jo. We might be needed sooner than you think.'

Jo was just about to ask her to explain, but she'd gone. What Judith had just said didn't make any sense to her at all. Bad vibes? Honestly. Spirit guides? Please. Byrd? Oh God she hoped so.

Jo went back to bed with a glimmer of hope that maybe her life wouldn't be so empty and cold for very much longer.

CHAPTER 14

The man who would become known as the Pumpkin Man was, as his name suggested, messing about with pumpkins. How he'd ever got the gig he'd no idea and frankly spending his time carving faces in pumpkins wasn't the best use of his talents. What talents, he had no idea, but he was sure he had some somewhere. It was just that he'd lost them along life's highway.

He'd ended up as a security guard, someone who felt important in a uniform, but was really ridiculed, lazy and underpaid. Security my arse. If the shop he worked for thought he was going to run after shoplifters, then they could think again. In a large chain store, catering to the young, cheap fashion buyers, the wear one season and then throw away brigade, trying to stop them shoplifting was a ridiculous notion. It went with the territory as far as he was concerned.

The kids shoplifted, skills learned from their parents no doubt, and he wasn't about to start strip searching young women who were wearing several outfits at once. Bloody hell he wasn't some sort of pervert. He was seriously considering giving up the bloody stupid job, but Christmas was coming. He'd a couple of kiddies to buy for, not that they lived with him. As soon as his wife realised her mistake by marrying him, understood that he'd amount to nothing, she threw him out of their Housing Association home and gaily embarked on relationships with a string of men, each one larger than the previous, all frightening the shit out of her ex-husband.

So there he was in a crummy bedsit, carving out pumpkins for another bloke who frightened the shit out of him. At least he was getting paid for his efforts. He'd also have the opportunity to have sex with three women that night. And that was nothing to be sniffed at he had to admit. The only sex he got these days was the kind you paid for. So to get three free chances to dip his wick, well he was in.

He'd lobbed the top off three pumpkins and was scooping out the innards as best he could. Once most of the seeds and flesh were out, he cut triangles in the body of the first pumpkin. Two for eyes and one for a nose. The jagged mouth grinned, but not in a nice way. There was nothing friendly about it. He'd also been given three cards and had been told to pin them on the pumpkins, leaving them in the girls' rooms, not forgetting to light the tea lights inside them before he left.

Barely able to contain his excitement, Pumpkin Man attacked the next one, determined to make the best pumpkin lanterns he could. Who knows, if he did well, he could get another gig out of this.

CHAPTER 15

As Halloween celebrations ratcheted up around Chichester, the Watcher sat atop the cathedral watching the comings and goings. The pubs and restaurants were opening and soon would be filled with excited customers drinking and eating too much but determined to have a good time. It was this lack of self-control that the Watcher was tapping into. It was going to be a busy night and he flicked out a forked tongue and licked his lips in anticipation.

His history went back to ancient times, before God sent his divine deluge to cleanse the earth. Once a guardian of the human race, he had lusted over their beautiful women. They were wonderous in form, delightful to be with and were as skilled as Eve at weaving their silken webs over men and keeping them forever in their thrall. And the Watcher and his fellow angels were certainly in their thrall.

And so, against their instructions, a few of them descended to earth, moved among men and coupled with their women. The fairer sex did not disappoint and the fallen enthusiastically imbued the human race with powers and knowledge far beyond their capabilities, by way of gifts for the welcome humans had given them. They taught their charges arts and technologies such as weaponry, cosmetics, mirrors, sorcery, and other techniques that would otherwise be discovered gradually over time by men, not foisted upon them all at once. In time their children were born, a race that was part human and part God, who were feared and respected and became the protectors of the angels and their women. However, others saw the offspring as savage giants who pillaged the earth and endangered humanity.

Eventually, God had had enough and smite the evil cities in his anger and revulsion, killing the children of the fallen and their mothers by a great flood. Only one man was spared, Noah. The Watchers were scattered to the wind and banished from the face of God and from his temples. This hardened the hearts of the Watchers and they, in turn, swore vengeance on God, and their long-suffering search for suitable women to help them fill the earth with their children once again, began.

CHAPTER 16

By late afternoon on the 31st October the Halloween celebrations were in full swing in Chichester. All the shops, restaurants and pubs in the city centre were decorated, vying with each other for the coolest, spookiest, most horrible windows. The children loved it. Running from one display to the other, oohing and aahing and screaming. Many of them were in fancy dress. Skeletons, witches, warlocks, and evil beings danced through the streets together. It was clear all the schools in the area had held fancy dress days and the children would stay in costume for the rest of the day and night, as they went trick or treating.

It should have been a happy sight, but for Jo, walking through the streets, it seemed to be a portent for disaster. Maybe it was just the memory of the bombing in the Italian restaurant just round the corner, where so many had died, including her close friend Judith. But she didn't think so. It was more wisps of feelings that darted around her. She tried to grab hold of them, but they always wriggled away. Taunting her. Dancing just out of reach. What was happening and where? She felt something but didn't have the words to explain it or describe it.

She slipped into a supermarket, intent on buying a few staples. But once there she still couldn't get away from Halloween. The store was decorated within an inch of its life and the music blaring from the speakers were all Halloween tunes. Wherever she turned there were grinning pumpkins, skeletons, witches. She felt cold air on the back of her neck and whirled round. Nothing. No one there. Then it happened again. What the hell was going on? She turned, intent on giving the joker who was playing with her a piece of her mind, when her phone rang.

Digging it out of her pocket, she saw it was Byrd. She pressed the button to answer the call. She wanted to tell him how she felt, that she was frightened and alone, was convinced she was being followed, being toyed with, but she didn't have time to speak.

'Jo, it's me,' he barked. 'There's been an attack on a young woman.'

'When?'

'A few minutes ago.'

'Where?'

Byrd gave her the address.

'I'm in the town centre. I'll meet you there.'

Jo killed the call, dropped her shopping basket on the floor and ran.

CHAPTER 17

The sight that confronted Jo was of a young woman in a sorry state. Her face was red and swollen, her clothes torn. Dark hair that appeared to be shoulder length looked like the stuff of nightmares, each hair seemed to be charged with static and was quite literally standing on end. The small bedroom appeared to be ransacked. The room smelled damp, old and rotten, almost putrid. She looked up at the walls and ceiling of the room, expecting them to be full of mould, but no. Which meant there was only one other smell like that. The smell from the morgue when they had a particularly old, decomposing body. It was liked Stilton cheese gone off, ripe and thick, the odour lingering in the air. Whatever had been in the bedroom that night had certainly made its mark.

Byrd was there, comforting the girl. For a moment Jo felt jealous. That was a ludicrous thought, but what could she do? His arms should be around her and not this... this... prostitute. She immediately felt awful. Even if the girl was a sex worker, it didn't mean she deserved Jo's derision, especially after what she appeared to have been subjected to. Jo thought it was a good job she hadn't articulated her thoughts and swallowed down her shame at her prejudice.

'Ah, Jo,' said Byrd. 'This is Suki. We're just waiting for the ambulance.'

'Hey, Suki,' said Jo. Squatting down in front of the girl she said, 'I'm DI Jo Wolfe and that rather handsome man with his arms around you is DS Eddie Byrd.' She wanted to take one of Suki's hands in her own, but daren't. Firstly, they could hold vital forensic evidence and Jo couldn't take the risk of contaminating it and secondly, she didn't want to have a 'reading' in front of Byrd. So she had to make do with smiling at the poor girl.

'Help is on its way,' she said, then looked at Byrd, her eyebrows raised in a question.

He nodded and spoke over the top of Suki's head. 'Uniforms are on their way to secure the scene. Bill is re-routing to here from another less urgent incident, to collect any forensic evidence. The hospital have been advised and will be ready to admit Suki as soon as she gets there.'

'Excellent. Thanks, Byrd. Suki? Can you tell me what happened?'

'Um, um, I'm a...' Suki tripped over the next word.

'Sex worker?' asked Jo helping her out.

Suki nodded. 'Just on the side, you know. Everything was normal to start with. I'd seen him around, the customer that is, so I felt fairly safe. None of the girls had reported any problems with him. But once he started, well it was as though he turned into someone else. Something else. He started clawing at me. Hurting me. Raping me.' Suki took a few ragged breaths. 'He refused to wear a condom. I told him that no condom meant no sex.' Suki sniffed. 'He said he'd do what he wanted, then he beat me up and r...r...raped me.'

Suki collapsed in tears. Turning her head she burrowed into Byrd's shoulder, muffling her sobs. God knows what her actions might be doing to any forensic evidence, but the girl was so very distressed. Jo's eyes met Byrd's. It was clear they both felt immensely sorry for the young girl.

The sound of heavy boots on the stairs made all three of them look up, just as a two-man paramedic crew burst through the door. Leaving Suki in their expert hands, Byrd assured her they would see her at Chichester Hospital later.

Running down the stairs, they were met by two uniformed officers. Byrd stationed one by the door into the street and one upstairs outside the door of Suki's flat. Then Byrd and Jo hurried to Byrd's car.

'Did you notice the pumpkin?' Jo asked when they'd climbed in.

'Not particularly, no. I saw there were Halloween decorations.'

'Here,' said Jo and passed him her mobile, open to a picture. In it a grinning pumpkin had something stuffed in its mouth. You could just about make out the writing: 'Look to the Book of Enoch.'

'What the hell?' said Byrd.

'Exactly,' replied Jo. 'I think our man left a message for us.'

CHAPTER 18

Jo and Byrd didn't speak on their short walk back to the police station. The night was drawing in and the temperature plummeting. Jo had her usual trouser suit on with flat shoes, and wool coat over the top, but was still cold. Whether that was from the weather or the scene they had left, Jo wasn't sure. Byrd was walking alongside her, arms swinging, focused and determined. She wanted to hold his hand, take his arm, anything. She was desperate for the easy familiar way they'd had between each other. But that was before. When they'd been a couple.

Jo had so much she wanted to say, but daren't. They'd reached some sort of impasse and she didn't want to jeopardise that. Entering the building, they nodded to Jed on the front desk and Byrd let them into the station by keying in the security code. Once inside, Byrd went to brief Sasha and Jill, while Jo went to see Harry Sykes.

'Boss?' Jo said after she'd knocked on the DCI's open door.

'Ah, Jo, come in. Leave the door open.'

'A new case has just come in.'

'Yes. The assault and rape of a young woman. Control have informed me.'

'Good. She's been taken to Chichester Hospital. Do my team take this one?'

'Anything urgent on at the moment?'

'No, Sir.'

Harry eyed her for a moment. 'Very well. Take it. Report back once you have more information.'

'Thank you, Sir,' Jo said as Sykes returned his attention to the papers on his desk.

The new Boss wasn't very chatty. Dour Yorkshire man definitely summed him up. Jo couldn't read him at all. Perhaps things would change once they were into the meat of this case.

Once Sykes was sure Jo had left his office, he raised his head, watching her walk down the corridor and back to Major Crimes. He wasn't sure what to make of her. She was very self-contained. Without doubt, good at solving crimes. The trouble was she seemed to work more on instinct than on hard evidence. At least that was the word around the station. No one really had a bad word to say about her, although some described her as, 'a bit of a cold fish'. But that was just those who resented the way new graduate officers could come straight into CID after a few years' experience in the 'real world'. Harry's view on that was that it was best to live and let live. Everyone had something different to bring to the party and that's how crimes were solved: by everyone pitching in and trying out new ideas, brainstorming motives and interpretation of the evidence. Not by individuals showboating. It was the case that was important. Less so the individuals. Unless, of course, it reflected badly on him. He'd climbed the ladder on the backs of those who had been unfortunate enough to be his subordinate and make a mistake.

Looking at Jo's file, Sykes realised he knew Jo's father. They'd briefly met on an investigation years ago when Mick had been in the Met. A serial killer had been roaming the country and a large task force had been set up that they were both part of. They were young detective constables, carrying out the leg work for higher ranking detectives. He could see Mick in Jo, of course. The same determination, enthusiasm for the job, total commitment to the police force.

Yes, he decided, his spell at Chichester was going to be very interesting indeed.

CHAPTER 18

Returning to the CID floor, Jo nodded at Byrd, to signal they'd been given the case. They grabbed their coats and made their way to the hospital.

Suki was lying in bed in a small side ward and she was the only occupant. The nurses had cleaned her wounds, which actually made the bruises, cuts and grazes look worse than they had earlier. The covering of blood had hidden what lay underneath. Her face was swollen, eyes barely open. There were black and red splotches all over her face. Her hands, lying on the white sheet, were also cut and bruised. On one hand every fingernail was broken, where Suki had clawed at something during the attack as she tried to escape.

'Hey,' said Jo as they approached the bed. 'How are you feeling now?'

Suki merely shrugged.

Jo tried again. 'Has someone been to check you over and do some forensic tests?' Jo meant a rape kit but was wary of using that term.

Suki nodded.

'We were wondering if you could help by telling us a little bit about yourself. You know, for background. You might have information that could help stop this happening to someone else.'

Suki looked up at Jo from under swollen eyelids. She had been scrunching the sheet in her right hand and stopped, smoothing it straight again. But, inevitably, she'd left behind an imprint, a set of lines where the material had been creased. A reminder of the trauma.

'Just you,' Suki whispered to Jo.

Byrd said, 'I'll just go and find the doctor,' and moved out of earshot to give Suki and Jo some privacy.

'I, um, I, um, I'm a student at Chichester Uni. I became a prostitute last year, because I couldn't afford to pay the rent and eat. It was an either or, really, the student loan just didn't cover everything. I was always broke. Never had enough food. Couldn't go out. My life was really crappy, you know?'

Jo nodded.

'I just couldn't find another option. Nothing else paid as well. I graduated earlier this year with a First and then decided to stay on to do a Masters.'

'Well done you,' said Jo. 'That's quite an achievement.'

Suki smiled, but it was clearly painful, and she winced. 'But it also meant I'd have to continue with, with, this...'

Tears ran down Suki's face and Jo's heart broke for her. Jo herself had been shielded from the cost of university, her family could well afford to pay the fees. But if they hadn't? Then she could have faced the same dilemma as Suki. Jo felt deeply embarrassed about her earlier judgemental attitude towards Suki when they'd first met.

'I love academia and education and always have. And

it will be the only way I can get out of doing sex work. It gives more opportunities for someone who doesn't have a lot, you know?" she said.

'You don't have to explain yourself to me, Suki. I'm not here to judge you, just to help you. But you have to help me, help you. Okay?'

Suki nodded.

'You need to tell me what happened.'

Suki's eye widened and she pushed herself back into the pillows propping her up. She shook her head. 'Not yet. Maybe later. I, I, can't. I just can't.' The tears that had dried started up again.

Jo took Suki's hand and squeezed it. 'It's alright, I understand.'

And in a flash Jo did understand.

Smiles, laughter and inuendo bagged the client for Suki and together they tripped up the stairs to her small bedsit. Once the formalities were over and Suki had placed the money in her cash box, they moved to the bed. He seemed to be enjoying himself, even though Suki felt nothing. But, hey, that was the name of the game. She hadn't realised what a good actress she could be. Let's face it Meg Ryan in 'When Harry Met Sally', had nothing on Suki. His features blurred. One face looked pretty much like another in her line of work. It's not like you gazed into a lover's eyes or anything. Quite the opposite. Suki hardly looked at the men. She was more interested in their money than their faces or bodies.

But then something changed. There was a definite shift in attitude. Something different. Something wrong. He roughly entered her, without a condom on.

'Hey,' she shouted, 'You can't do that.'

'I'll do what the hell I want.'

Suki wondered why his voice had changed. It was

deeper, angrier, rougher. She bucked her hips, trying to get him off her, but it only spurred him on.

Before she knew it, she was flipped over and dragged to the edge of the bed, legs splayed. There was a hand on her neck and one on her back. She was penetrated again. Both hands were now around her neck. He squeezed until her vision went blurry, then grabbed her hair, pulling her head backwards. He screamed as he climaxed, howled in ecstasy, then fell on top of her, forcing the air out of her lungs. She couldn't breathe. Began to panic.

The rank smell of his breath near her ear made her want to throw up. It was as if every tooth in his mouth was rotting, loose in the mangled mess of his gums. 'Now be a good girl and I'll leave you alone,' he rasped. 'But tell anyone and our next encounter won't be nearly as pleasant.'

Jo stifled a scream of her own and pulled her hand away. It felt hot and she had pins and needles, radiating out from her palm. Kneading it with her right hand she looked at Suki. Something passed between them. A look of understanding. Suki's eyes pleaded with Jo, who nodded in return. She'd find the bastard and try to make Suki whole again.

'I promise,' Jo whispered and went to find Byrd.

He was by the nursing station on the phone. Jo heard him say, 'Very well, Sir.'

Pocketing the mobile, he saw Jo and said, 'We've another one.'

Jo raised an eyebrow.

'But this time she's dead.'

'Where?'

'A flat near the town centre.'

Jo nodded and they ran for the stairs.

Once in the car, with Byrd driving, she pulled out her

mobile and called Jill. Quickly bringing her up to speed she then said, 'Work with Sasha, get as much information as you can on known sex offenders, where they live, known associates, rapists active in the area.'

'Yes, Boss,' said Jill. 'Where will you be?'

'Body found in the Lewis Road area. Byrd and I are heading there now.'

'Sasha's just handed me a note,' said Jill. 'It looks like the DCI is on his way to you.'

Great. Just what Jo needed. 'Thanks, Jill.'

Jo ended the conversation. Byrd looked at her, eyebrows raised.

'Looks like our dour Yorkshireman is about to cut his teeth on our dead girl.'

CHAPTER 20

The property Byrd pulled up in front of, was very central - located in Lewis Road, just a few minutes' walk from the University campus. It was in a well-lit and safe area within in easy reach of the town centre.

Chichester's historic heart and affluent community, plus its proximity to beautiful countryside, made it an ideal location for those wanting the best of both urban and rural living. But every city has a student quarter and Chichester's centred around Lewis Road. It was very popular with student sharers. The houses were mostly terraced many from social housing stock that was bought by the tenants under the Right to Buy scheme. The lucky students got a nice refurbished property. However, those not so quick off the mark found there were only tired properties in need of some general updating, left. Some were owned by Landlords that couldn't be bothered with the general upkeep of the houses. They just collected the rent and then suddenly became uncontactable when things went wrong. The good properties went first, to those students with the funds to be able to pay for them from June, even though the Autumn Term didn't start until nearly October.

The house Jo and Byrd went to was in the latter category. Uniformed police officers had already arrived and set up a cordon down the street and were moving residents out of those houses in the immediate area. As Jo looked around, she mostly saw frightened young women dressed in clothing thrown on for warmth or comfort. Three young women in tears were huddled around the open back of an ambulance.

'Looks like the other residents of the house,' Jo said to Byrd. 'We'll talk to them after we've viewed the scene. Just makes sure they don't go anywhere would you?'

As Byrd moved away, Jo shrugged her way into protective clothing. Stood by the front door, she took a deep breath, trying to prepare herself for what lay ahead. Viewing murder scenes never got any easier, she decided. Maybe the day they all merged into one another and she stopped feeling anything, well that would be the day she left the force. But that was still a long way off. While she had the determination to protect the people of Chichester in particular, and West Sussex in general, she would carry on with her mission. At times it was a very heavy burden, especially since the escalation of her 'gift'. Jo had only just recovered her equilibrium from her vision of Suki's attack and now she was being thrust back into another heart-wrenching crime scene. At least Suki was lucky, Jo reflected. She was still alive.

Once Byrd joined her and was ready in his own protective garb, he gave Jo details of the dead girl. 'We think her name is Tess,' he said. 'A student at Chichester Uni who is a prostitute on the side. Same story as Suki, she needed the money to be able to continue with her studies. Aged 20, from Norfolk.'

'Oh God,' said Jo. 'Come on, let's do this,' and they proceeded into the house, their features and characteristics made androgynous by the outfits they wore. Jo thought someone would be hard pressed to tell which was which. Masks covered their faces, hoods covered all their hair, bulky plastic suits did nothing for their body shape and gloves and bootees covered their hands and feet. All obscuring any defining features.

They moved into the house and slowly climbed the stairs, suits rustling at every step. The stairs were narrow and steep, and Jo held onto the railing as she climbed, although that didn't seem very stable, wobbling perilously under her grasp. Once on the landing, they were called forward by Bill, towards the back bedroom. Sliding their way in past him, they both stood against the wall, looking at, but not touching, the crime scene.

A young woman, who the housemates believed was Tess, was sprawled, face downward across the bed, with legs dangling onto the floor. The bottom half of her body was naked, and the top half covered in part by a ripped blouse and a tattered bra. She looked like a broken life-sized doll or marionette, disjointed and lifeless. She'd been wearing a white wig, which was slipping off her head revealing mousy brown hair underneath.

'Do we know what Tess was wearing tonight?'

'The girls weren't sure about the clothes, but all three said she was wearing her white wig. It was her trademark, if you like. She always wore it when she was 'on the job' as they put it,' said Byrd.

Jo nodded. 'Looks like that's her then. When we get back out in the street, see if the girls have contact details for Tess' family. Otherwise we'll have to wait for forensics to finish with her room.'

'Yes, Boss.'

The pathologist, Jeremy Grogan, was stood by the body and looked up as they filed in. 'There is obvious evidence of a particularly vicious attack,' he said, not bothering with a greeting. 'She was raped. The attacker wasn't wearing a condom, as you can see tracks of semen down her thighs.'

'How did she die?' Jo asked, although she was pretty sure she knew.

'Strangled, is my initial impression. She's got bruising to her neck.'

'Maybe he didn't mean to kill her,' said Byrd. 'After all, Suki's still alive.'

'My thoughts too,' agreed Jo.

'I'm pretty sure it's the same attacker,' said Bill, who had processed Suki's room after Jo and Byrd had left.

'Because?'

'Because when I arrived, the lights were off in the room. There was flickering candlelight from that Halloween pumpkin, over there on the other side of the bed. Just like the last one. Oh and there's a message pinned to it.'

Jo manoeuvred her way past Jeremy and approached the pumpkin. Sure enough there was a note pinned to it. Jo squatted down and then read aloud, 'And it came to pass when the children of men had multiplied that in those days were born unto them beautiful and comely daughters. And the angels, the children of the heaven, saw and lusted after them, and said to one another: Come, let us choose us wives from among the children of men and beget us children.'

CHAPTER 21

Jo and Byrd got out of the room and left the house. As they emerged into the night, Harry Sykes was just suiting up.

'Sir,' Jo acknowledged.

'Ah, Jo and Eddie. I'm just going to take a look at the scene. Wait for me here.'

A bit abrupt, but Jo gave her boss the benefit of the doubt. After all he was going to view a dead body. But Jo resented the instruction all the same.

While they waited, she showed Byrd the photograph with the message on.

'It's a lot longer than the first,' Byrd said.

'Yes, I wonder why?'

'Is it tied in with the first, then? This Book of Enoch.'

'I guess so. I've sent Sasha and Jill a photo of the message and they are working on that back at the office.'

'Are we thinking its biblical?'

'I'd say so, but I don't remember the Book of Enoch being in the bible.'

'Didn't know you were religious, Boss.'

Jo grinned. 'You know damn well I'm not, Eddie. Spiritual maybe. Religious? Not a chance.'

'Neither am I,' said a voice.

'Neither are you what, Sir?' said Jo as Sykes walked up to them.

'Religious. Are you thinking it's some nut job trying to rid Chichester of fallen women?'

'No, that doesn't feel right,' said Byrd. 'I'm more inclined to think the death of our girl here is more of an accident. Otherwise Suki would be dead as well.'

'Good point, Sergeant,' said Sykes. 'What about this message?'

'I've sent it over to Sasha to work on while we're here.'

'Good. Let me know if anything else urgent comes in.'

'Yes, Sir. Where will you be?' asked Jo.

Sykes looked at his watch. 'It's 9pm. I'm off home.'

As they watched Sykes walk away Byrd said, 'Maybe he's still got unpacking to do?'

'Or maybe he's just pulling rank. Reminding us that it's our job to do the leg work.' Either way Jo wasn't impressed. Alex Crooks hadn't been the most gifted of investigators, but at least he'd cared. He'd given all to the job and it cost him his marriage and ultimately his life. Jo wasn't sure she could say the same for Sykes.

CHAPTER 22

It was 11pm, perilously close to the witching hour, when Jo's mobile buzzed. She'd only been home for half an hour and she knew she should have been in bed, but was too wired to sleep and so had been building her own crime scene wall at home. Not that it was helping any. But then again, it was forcing her to recognise some of the similarities of the two scenes. The obvious ones of the pumpkin, the messages and positioning of the body which was the same way that Suki had been violated.

She had been halfway to the fridge to pour a glass of white wine which might help her sleep she'd reasoned, when she answered the call. Once she knew the reason behind it, she was thankful she'd only drunk herbal tea so far that night. There had been another attack, in close proximity to the other one on Lewis Road. The residents were in an uproar. Uniformed reinforcements were on their way, as the crowds were swelling and threatening to break through the cordons.

Flying through the streets in her red Mini Cooper, Jo's imagination was running wild. Or maybe not. It seemed that the pumpkin man, as she was beginning to think of him, had struck again. Three rapes in one night. She hoped to God this would be the last one, as their killer certainly seemed to have an affinity with Halloween. She couldn't see the 1st of November having the same pull for him, as the 31st October did. At least she hoped not.

Jo pulled up at her third crime scene of the night, 15 minutes after leaving the house. A personal record for her. It was a good job she was in effect in a plain clothes police car, having had blues and twos fitted for just such occasions. Oh and she'd had to take the Advanced Driver's Course, which she'd thoroughly enjoyed. Rather too much, according to her father, who turned a peculiar shade of puce when her passenger.

The ambulance crew were getting ready to transport the girl to hospital when Jo arrived. Byrd gave her the salient points of the case as they waited in the street. 'Storm is aged 20, a sex worker on the side, as she puts it. The same story, she augments her student loans with her earnings as a prostitute.'

'What state is she in?'

'Pretty bad. She was beaten about the face and body and forcibly penetrated without a condom. The poor girl is terrified of having been given Aids or other such diseases. The paramedics don't think any bones are broken, but she's being taken in for treatment and a rape kit.'

'Can she describe who did this to her?'

'Not really, she was mumbling something about the fact that her client seemed to change halfway through.'

'Change?'

Byrd nodded. 'Yes, she said it was a though one person went back to her room with her, but a different one altogether raped her.'

'And a pumpkin? Is there one?'

'Yes, here's a picture of it.'

Byrd handed Jo his mobile and she read:

'I have begotten a strange son, different and unlike man, and resembling the sons of the God of Heaven; and his nature is different and he is not like us, and his eyes are as the rays of the sun, and his face is glorious.'

'What the hell does that mean?'

'To be honest, Boss, I've no bloody idea. Oh, here comes Storm.'

Jo approached the back of the ambulance and smiled down at the girl on the gurney. She seemed covered in bruises and her face under the oxygen mask was bloody, her lips gashed and bleeding.

Jo leaned down to speak into her ear. 'My name's Jo and I'm going to find the beast who did this to you. I'll see you at the hospital after you've been examined. Okay?'

The girl managed a small nod, more a blink of an eyelid than a movement of her head.

Jo turned away and had a coughing fit as she returned to Byrd.

'You okay?' he asked.

Jo nodded, then gasped a couple of deep breaths.

'What the hell was that smell coming off Storm? It was as though she'd been rolling in a compost heap, or cow dung. Bloody hell.' She fished a handkerchief out of her pocket and spat into it, trying to get the taste of it out of her mouth.

'You'll need something under your nose when we go up to her room.'

'That bad?'

'That bad,' Byrd confirmed and Jo walked reluctantly after him as they went to dress in protective clothing.

Once upstairs, Bill and his one assistant were busy lifting prints and taking samples and photographs.

'We've not removed anything yet,' Bill told Jo. 'I thought you'd want to see the scene first.'

Jo nodded. 'Thanks, Bill, could you give us a minute?'

They moved out of the way so Jo and Byrd could enter. The room was only a small double. With a bed pushed into the corner, a pine chest of drawers and a wonky wardrobe in an alcove, it felt crammed. Byrd had been right about the smell. Jo wanted to throw up and then throw open a window but knew she couldn't compromise the crime scene.

'It's the same as before,' Byrd said. 'Storm was subdued by being beaten there on the bed.'

Jo could see numerous patches of blood on the duvet cover. There was also some blood spatter on the wall. 'What the hell was she hit with?'

'Well that's the thing, she said she thought it was just his fists. She doesn't remember a weapon.'

'If that's the case our suspect's hands will be a mess. And the pumpkin?'

'Storm insists it's not hers. She doesn't know how it got there. But she thought the customer might have had a bag with him.'

'Really?'

'Yeah, so she says.'

Jo filed that one away, to be examined later. Pumpkins don't just appear out of thin air. Although Jo knew there were stranger things than that in the world and she'd encountered some of them. Her scalp prickled at the thought that the Pumpkin Man might not be a man at all.

'Okay, I've seen enough. Thanks, Bill, you can finish up now.'

Bill nodded and went back to work.

Jo and Byrd disrobed and then he asked, 'What next?'

Jo had to decide between visiting the mortuary or visiting Storm. She chose the living over the dead. After all, the body wasn't going anywhere and she didn't want Storm to suddenly disappear before they'd talked to her.

'The hospital to see Storm. Come on, follow me in your car.'

CHAPTER 23

They found the young girl in a private room at Chichester hospital, weeping softly and dabbing delicately at her tears, as the skin on her face was no doubt very sore, being swollen, full of scratches and cuts.

'Hi, Storm,' Jo said. 'Remember me? I'm Jo and this is Eddie Byrd.'

Storm nodded and sniffed.

'Do you know who did this to you?'

She nodded.

Jo took a deep breath trying to calm herself. It couldn't be this easy could it?

'A bloke called John.'

Jo's heart sank and she shared a secret smile with Byrd. Oh well.

But then Storm said, 'John Holt. He lives near me.'

'Has he been a client before?' said Byrd.

'Yes,' nodded Storm. 'That's why I don't understand what happened. He's never been like… like… this!' Storm's weeping escalated to crying.

'Storm, where near you? It's really important.'

She sniffed but looked at Byrd. 'Alexandra Road don't know what number, but it's one of the nicer looking houses opposite the park. It's been renovated and made into flats and bedsits.'

'Thanks,' Jo said and patted Storm's hand as it lay on the sheet.

The scene flashed in front of Jo's eyes and seared itself on the back of her eyelids. She stifled a scream at the suddenness of it all. She saw Storm's small bedroom. She was with her client on the bed. But that wasn't what had caught Jo's attention. There was a large body, or form, or something, hovering over Storm and John, as though dangling from the ceiling by hidden wires, or rope, or something. Whatever it was, nothing like that should have been in Storm's bedroom. It filled the ceiling, ripples coursing through its body, pulsing, growing stronger with each beat. Fear ran down Jo's spine and her breath came in fast spurts. She could feel the evil emanating from the being.

In her vision she shouted, to warn Storm, but of course that didn't work. She was a bystander, a documenter, not a participant. Then, with a roar, the being dropped down and entered the man on the bed with Storm, who was presumably John Holt. Jo watched as the two became one. She felt so sorry for poor Storm. She hadn't stood a chance against whoever it was, whatever it was. The best description of it that Jo could come up with was black. Which didn't help at all. She just had the impression of a black coat and large black hat and for some reason she was reminded of a scarecrow, those things that sat in the fields in the spring, unnoticed by humans but a deterrent against the birds, who viewed him as human.

Jo had seen enough. She pulled her hand back, managed a small smile at Storm and hurried to catch up with Byrd. She wasn't at all sure she liked this escalation in her gift (or curse, definitely a curse at the moment). She'd had more control when it was just the last thoughts and actions of the dead. But now, being able to read from living human beings, well Jo wasn't so sure she liked that at all. She kept being ambushed by her gift and she felt like she had no control over it. Maybe she needed to talk this through with Keith Thomas, her guide and teacher in the spiritualist church.

But that was for another day. For now they needed to catch this John Holt.

Jo hurried after Byrd, all thoughts of going home for the night banished. It looked like they would be pulling an all-nighter. First, they needed to speak to Storm's doctor and then try and find John Holt.

CHAPTER 24

Abbey struggled awake. She'd been having a dream about being on the water. Swimming in it? She didn't think so. Walking by it? Yes, maybe, that sounded better. She was walking along a tow path somewhere., She didn't know where and then she'd slipped. Her foot had slid away from her and she landed with a thump, not on the tow path, but in the water. How strange! Even stranger, she could still feel the water. She was sitting in puddles of it. The bed felt drenched.

Not knowing if she was awake or dreaming, Abbey put her hands beneath the duvet and felt around. The bed was wet. It wasn't just a dream. She really was sitting in water. Oh my God! Water! Her waters had broken. She'd been watching television in bed and nodded off during the news. She had to get to hospital, she knew that. But how? It didn't seem right to call an ambulance, there must be another way.

Abbey swung her legs off the bed and sat on the edge. She was in no pain yet. She was just wet through. Thinking back to the baby book she'd been reading, there was no immediate danger, to either her or the baby, but she should make her way to the hospital to prevent any infection while her labour progressed. Stripping off her sopping tee-shirt and knickers, she managed to clamber her way into a new pair of pants and slip a maternity dress over her head. Feeling better already, she grabbed her mobile. Perhaps she should call a taxi. But she didn't want to rush there just yet.

Abbey thought of Edith and her promise to be with her at the birth if that's what Abbey wanted. Abbey hadn't been sure at the time, but as reality hit, of course Abbey wanted Edith with her. She was the only person Abbey knew that she could really call a friend. And, if she was honest, Abbey was frightened. Alright, bloody terrified, she admitted to her bedroom, but no one could know that. Picking up her mobile she called Edith, who seemed particularly awake. Abbey had expected to wake her up, but Edith sounded as though she wasn't anywhere near tired and promised to be round in a jiffy in the car.

'The car?' Abbey asked stupidly. 'I didn't know you had a car.'

'Doesn't everyone?'

'Well, no.' Certainly not people like Abbey at any rate. Still, thank goodness for Edith. 'What would I do without you?' Abbey said, feeling herself getting emotional. She was definitely unbalanced, had lost her equilibrium. She was in unknown territory, that was all it was, at least she hoped so. She sniffed back tears.

'Let's not worry about that, eh? The thing is, I am here for you and we're in this together. I'll be round in five minutes.'

Abbey tried to thank Edith, but something got in the way. A tightening in her stomach. A band that was made of pain, pushing away all other thoughts and feelings and threatening to overwhelm her, like waves constantly crashing over her head. She struggled to breathe. Her legs trembled. She stumbled her way back to the bed and sat with a thump. She managed to ride the wave of pain that roared over her, leaving her gasping for breath and struggling to stay upright. She hoped Edith would be there soon, as she passed out on the bed.

The next thing Abbey remembered was a nurse saying, 'Come on, Abbey, deep breaths, in with the gas and air.' Abbey sucked at it greedily as the pain hit, although it was more in hope than actuality. It was like smoking a cigarette that didn't have any nicotine in it no matter how hard you dragged on it. Abbey realised she was in the Maternity Unit at Chichester Hospital, but she'd no real recollection of getting there. She supposed it didn't matter. All that mattered was that her baby was being born.

'How far along did you say you were?' the midwife asked Abbey.

'Thirty-two weeks.'

'Really? Looks more like full term to me. Boy or girl?'

'Boy.'

'Well, he's a big one, that's for sure.'

'Big?'

'Yes, and, oh my goodness the head's crowning now. Abbey, the baby's coming, but he's big. We're going to have to cut you. Okay?'

Abbey couldn't remember what that meant, but she was happy to agree to anything if it got rid of this agonising pain. She couldn't get away from it. It was the most horrendous thing she'd ever felt. She thought she was going to die. She grabbed Edith's hand and squeezed with all her might as she was told to push. Abbey screamed out her anguish. Screamed the baby out of her body. Everything was happening at once and much faster than she'd expected it too. She thought it was supposed to take hours and hours for your first child to be born. She'd heard of stories of your first labour possibly lasting 24 hours. It looked like Abbey would be lucky to last one hour.

Everyone was bustling around the room and she could feel the tension in the air, it was as though there was something wrong.

'Sorry,' Abbey panted when she was on the other side of the latest wave. 'I hope I'm not hurting you.'

'I'm stronger than I look, dear,' said Edith. 'Don't you worry about me.'

But Abbey was in the throes of yet another contraction and being urged to push by the midwife. One final strain, a blood curdling scream and more pain than Abbey thought it was possible to survive... and the baby was born.

Two floors below, Jo and Byrd were just waiting for the doctor who had examined Storm. *At the precise moment Abbey was having her child, Jo felt it. She didn't know what it was. What had caused it. Just that there was a disturbance in the air. The lights flickered. Something made Jo rock back on her heels. Was the floor moving or was she moving? She felt disoriented. Something had disturbed the fabric of the world. The thin veil between this world and the next had a tear in it. She didn't know how she knew, but she did. Something momentous had just happened.*

She had this feeling of being watched. But there was nothing, there was no one there, at least not that she could see. But she could feel something, someone.

Looking around her, no one else appeared to have noticed anything. The staff were going about their business with precise movements. If anyone felt anything, they were refusing to acknowledge it, to be rushed, or to be panicked. Byrd seemed oblivious. He was doing something with his phone, head bent over the screen. Jo recognised this as one of his newly acquired avoidance tactics, so he wouldn't have to interact with her, or look into her eyes. She'd have to ask Judith when she next saw her, if she knew anything about it. It struck her as an absurd thought, on the face of it. That Jo would ask her friend when she next saw her. Her dead friend. A couple of months ago Jo would have dismissed such thoughts as madness. But now... now not so much.

'Well done, Abbey,' someone called from the general direction of her legs. 'It's a beautiful baby boy, 10 lbs at only 32 weeks, eh?'

'Is that normal?' Abbey began to wonder. No one had given her the baby yet. Where was he? What where all these people hiding?

'Of course it is, dear,' said Edith. 'Babies don't conform. They are what they are, and they are who they are. Look, here he is. He's absolutely beautiful. He's got 10 fingers and 10 toes and lots of lovely dark hair.'

At last someone put the baby into Abbey's waiting arms. He was wrapped in a blanket and someone had sponged his face clean. Abbey gazed at her son with adoring eyes. Edith was right, he was absolutely beautiful.

But it seemed the midwife was determined to have the last word. 'Date of birth, 31st October. Time of birth 11.55 pm. Fancy having your baby on Halloween, Abbey.

Have you a name yet?'

'Damien,' said Abbey.

'Oh,' gasped Edith. 'How lovely. Thank you, Abbey.'

'It was Edith's father's name.'

'Cool,' said the young midwife. 'Although with that combination, I hope it's not a bad omen.'

'What?' Abbey said. 'What are you talking about?'

'Don't you take any notice,' said Edith interrupting and patting Abbey's arm. 'I think it's a wonderful name, striking and different. Just like you, his mother, my dear.'

'Oh, Edith, thank you. I'm so lucky to have you in my life. And just as soon as I get this little one into a routine, we'll sort out where we're going with the business.'

'Don't worry about that, I'll keep an eye on the business, you just concentrate on this little one here.'

'This big one, you mean,' laughed Abbey, not realising how prophetic her words would turn out to be.

CHAPTER 25

John Holt hurried home. He was dishevelled, felt dirty and more importantly was afraid. He couldn't believe what had happened that night. He'd innocently thought that three girls in one night and carved pumpkins were all just a Halloween prank, but it seemed the prank had been played on him. He pulled his keys out of his pocket at his front door and fumbling for the right one, dropped them. Oh crap. He bent down and picked them up. Taking a hurried look over his shoulder he then rammed the key home. As he turned it and the door moved under his hand, he was so very grateful. For there was something unbelievably bad in Chichester that night and John had the feeling that whatever it was, it would be coming for him next.

Hurrying through the flat, he took off his coat, dropped it on the floor and grabbed a bottle of whisky. Not stopping to find a glass, he drank straight from the bottle. He spluttered as the fiery liquid burned his throat but persisted and swallowed. Then took another gulp. His nerves were shattered. What the hell had just happened? One minute he'd been giving Suki one and the next? He wasn't sure what the next was. Something fell from the ceiling. Something covering him, taking him over, making him someone he wasn't. His body had been used, as insane as that sounded. Not once, but three times! Holy crap.

The police would be coming for him. He was known in Chichester after all. Had a bit of a sheet from his younger days. But the girls all knew him. Gave him freebies every now and again when he had no money and a need in him for some company. They were good girls really. And this is how he repaid them? He took another gulp of whisky.

He stilled at a sound. A footstep above him? Then another. Was it outside, or inside? Was it neighbours, or something more malevolent? Was it upstairs or downstairs? His imagination was running riot. He saw pumpkins at every turn, ghostly figures outside the windows, chains clanking, wind whistling.

He whirled around. He could feel something. Some being, some entity, some... then the lights went out. John screamed at the suddenness of it. He was blind. Couldn't see a thing. But he could hear. Oh yes, he could hear. Scraping. Rustling. Dragging. And feel. Felt hands clutching at him. Pulling him this way and that. Roaming all over him. In his terror he thought he was going to have a heart attack. There were pains in his chest, down his arm, shortness of breath. He was going to die; he was sure of it. His eyes bulged, trying to see into the darkness. To see what was in the room with him.

Slowly his eyesight sharpened, getting used to the blackness. Nothing was ever completely dark in town, there were streetlights, car lights, the moon, any number of things. He could see shadows outside the window. He pawed the table and found his bottle of whisky. He looked around, but there was no one there. It was as if the feeling of someone pawing at him had been a figment of his imagination. But deep down he knew it wasn't. Unscrewing the cap he took a quick hit, then kept hold of the bottle. He figured that if he was attacked, he could always use it as a weapon.

John wasn't a brave man. He was pretty nondescript really. A sad bastard in a uniform that meant nothing. He was certain that he was about to die. He wondered if anyone would miss him. Be upset that he was gone. But he couldn't really think of anyone.

He felt behind him, found his chair and sat on it, as the darkness settled over him like a blanket. But there was nothing warm and comforting about it. He struggled to breathe. He was gasping for air. There was something over his face, over his body, squeezing the air out of his lungs and not letting anymore in. He tried and tried to find oxygen, but there was none to be had. He found he couldn't move his arms or his legs, he was pinned down by someone or something unknown.

Unable to breathe, unable to scream, John Holt, sad bastard, died as his heart gave out.

CHAPTER 26

Despite the lateness of the hour, Byrd and Jo hurried to John Holt's house. Byrd had got the house number from control, who confirmed the man had a criminal record, but it was mostly for petty thefts when he was much younger, nothing major, nothing to bring him to the attention of Jo and Byrd. Until now.

At Jo's request Byrd had also arranged for some uniformed police to attend, in case there was a scene to be secured. Jo seemed to think there would be. She said she had the feeling that John Holt would be dead.

There being no answer to their knock and as the door opened at Byrd's touch, they went in. Stood in the hall they could hear voices. Then music. It was the television, not people, so they followed the noise to the living room. Holt was sprawled in a chair in front of the television. Byrd quickly checked for a pulse but shook his head at Jo. There was nothing. The man was dead. Holt looked peaceful, as though he had just fallen asleep in front of the TV as many people did night after night. But this was one sleep he would not awaken from.

His hair was dishevelled, his skin pale. He was dressed in a cheap polo shirt that had at one time been white and was now a mucky grey. Trainers that had seen better days were on his feet, the white leather cracked and scuffed. Dark trousers were hitched up to reveal his ankles and legs. He looked in a sorry state. Jo put him in his 50's, his white and grey stubble peppering his face, which was pock marked from teenage acne. On the table was a pile of money peeking out of a brown envelope.

She called Jeremy Grogan. 'Sorry J, I need you again.'

'Bloody hell, Jo, what are you doing tonight? Is this some sort of Halloween special, or maybe a let's get Jeremy night?'

Jo had to smile. 'No practical jokes, not tonight, mate, we really do have a body.'

'What state is he in?'

Jo could hear Jeremy collecting keys, shrugging into a coat and clipping closed his case. 'Well, that's the thing. There's no obvious sign as to how he died. He's just sat in his chair as though he were watching television. At least, it was on when we entered the room. We haven't moved him, obviously we'll wait for you. But there's no bullet wound, knife wound, no spilt blood, he's just dead. It's like he just fell asleep.'

'And didn't wake up.'

'Yes.'

'Maybe that's the case? Why are you interested in him anyway?'

'He's our suspect in a triple rape!'

'What? All at once?'

'No, one at a time, you fool, three different women.'

'Crickey, he sounds like a right Don Juan.'

'No, afraid not, just someone with money,' and her gaze once more fell on the envelope full of bank notes.

Was that John's pay-off? Was that why he'd done it? Put those three girls through such an awful ordeal? She shook her head and turned away.

'Let's wait for Jeremy outside,' she said to Byrd and went to get some fresh air and to get away from the cloying atmosphere of the house. She could smell undertones of rot and decomposition in the closed room, as though John Holt had already begun to decay.

CHAPTER 27

Jo yawned her way into work later that morning at 9am. Byrd had gone to the post-mortems of first their dead girl, Tess, and then John Holt.

Sasha had made enquiries of the cathedral staff to see if anyone could help them with the cryptic references that had been pinned to the pumpkins and a young curate, Osian Price, was coming in later that morning to talk to them about The Book of Enoch. Apparently, he had made a study of it for his theology degree so the Bishop thought he would be the most suitable member of the clergy available to help.

Jo, not knowing what to expect, not having been in the Cathedral very much herself, even though she particularly enjoyed sitting in the gardens, was rather taken aback by the normalcy of the cleric. She had been envisaging someone like Father Brown, the eponymous crime-solving Roman Catholic priest in the BBC TV period drama. That black-garbed priest was in his 50's, sported round wired glasses, wore a black hat and carried the ubiquitous black umbrella, which he used to get himself out of scrapes. Osian was quite a different fish altogether. Younger, fresh faced, with black curly hair, eager and full of energy, he burst into the office, introduced himself to everyone, shaking their hands in turn, even Sasha's.

'So, how can I help?' he asked them.

'Could you tell us about the Book of Enoch?'

'Certainly, what do you want to know?'

'Well,' said Jo, 'we don't want an essay, or a theological discussion. We want clear information, a synopsis I suppose.'

Osian nodded. 'Sure, I'll try my best, if it gets too confusing just shout. OK? Can I ask why you want to know about the Book of Enoch?'

'Tell us about it first. We'll get to that later.'

'So,' Osian began, 'when the Book of Enoch was found in the Dead Sea Scrolls, it became clear that it was a piece of literature that had influenced biblical writers of the time, including those who wrote the New Testament.'

'Dead Sea Scrolls?' asked Jo.

'Manuscripts dating from the last three centuries BC and the first century AD. They were found in caves near the Dead Sea by archaeologists in the 1940's and 50's.'

'So the Book of Enoch was important?' asked Jo. Like the others she'd heard of The Dead Sea Scrolls but had no idea what they were.

'Yes, at least it was thought so at the time.'

'So why isn't that particular book in the modern bible?'

Jo thought Sasha must really want to know, to actually instigate a conversation. Was it possible that working for them, and being accepted for who she was without any pressure, Sasha could feel confident enough to come out of the protective shell she had wrapped herself in for fear of being ridiculed?

'Good question,' said Osian. 'Today it is only included in the main canons of Ethiopian Orthodox sects but it was popular for hundreds of years in ancient Jewish perspectives. In fact, some people have pointed out that it was likely the inspiration for the Book of Genesis, due to a number of similarities between the two.

'So, in the book, we find the story of Enoch. Now, he was the father of Methuselah and grandfather of Noah. I guess you've all heard of him! Enoch lived for 365 years up until the great flood that wiped out much of the population. Enoch was taken away in a fiery chariot before the great floods by the Archangel Michael, who some have interpreted as being extra-terrestrial. Could that fiery chariot actually have been a spacecraft powered by jet-engine?'

'Okay, you were doing really well there, Osian. Then you lost me with talk of extra-terrestrials and spaceships. Are we really supposed to take that seriously?' Jo asked.

'Well, I guess that's up to you. But historical writings strongly suggest that was what was believed at the time.'

Jo blew out a breath. 'Alright, well carry on, please.'

'The book that details the story of Enoch is extensive with over 100 chapters dispersed throughout several books, detailing accounts of the Nephilim and the Watchers.'

'I've never heard of those before,' said Jill.

'Ah, well,' Osian smiled, 'these giants, known as the Nephilim, are also described in the Book of Genesis. The giants are said to have been the children of angels, known as the Watchers, and female humans. Some believe that these giant beings may have been the reason for the great flood, as they were seen to be unnatural and harmful to the human race. That is the traditional biblical stance.'

'And the non-traditional?' asked Jo who was beginning to feel decidedly unnerved by what she was hearing. Talk of beings called Watchers and giant offspring was chilling her blood.

'There are theories that suggest our ancient ancestors were visited by a race from another planet. They point to the Watchers as the most likely to be those ancient astronauts. At the time, they were looked upon as angels, some good and some bad, who eventually procreated with select female humans'

'And was that good or bad?' Byrd asked.

Jo hadn't realised Byrd had joined them.

'What?'

'Procreating with humans?'

'Oh, I see, very bad. That's why they became known as the fallen angels.'

Jo saw that Byrd was looking very sceptical, Jill looked fascinated and Sasha was trying to carry on working surreptitiously.

'Can you confirm that these three messages are quotes from The Book of Enoch?'

Osian took the paper Jo was holding out and quickly scanned the contents.

'Oh yes, without question. I brought a copy of the Book of Enoch for you. I thought you might find it useful.'

'Thank you so much, Osian,' Jo said. 'Could you give it to Jill. Now as my colleague has just returned from two post-mortems and needs to tell us the findings, I'm afraid we're going to have to cut this short, for now at least.'

'Oh, right, I see.'

Jo wasn't sure that he did. Like all academics he could probably talk about his chosen subject, the Book of Enoch, all day. He looked just the kind that would enter

Mastermind, with the Book of Enoch as his chosen subject. Jo pushed away such fanciful thoughts as the theme music of the television show filled her head and said, 'Perhaps we could contact you again if we need to?' The harsh notes of the music in her head sounding more and more melodramatic.

'Yes, absolutely.'

'Lovely. Jill, could you take the Curate back to reception?'

Jill nodded and moved away, but not before Jo caught Jill blushing and smiling shyly at Osian Price, and Price placing his arm across Jill's back as he let her lead him to the lifts. Well I never, thought Jo, not having seen such a reaction from her young DC before. Normally Jill was quiet, reserved, very hard working and determined to keep her place in Major Crimes. Not that that meant she couldn't have a private life, but Jo knew only too well that once you joined the Police Force, your private life pretty much went out of the window. The Force had the highest divorce rate of all the services. You had to have a pretty special partner who could understand the total dedication it took to be a copper and the destructive effect it could have on relationships and family life.

After they'd gone, Jo looked at Byrd. For a moment sadness clouded her thoughts. Was Byrd her special partner? The one person who would understand the job and its demands? At one time she had thought so, but not now. Jo said, 'Did you hear all that, Byrd?'

Byrd nodded. 'And how does that help us, Boss?'

'I'm not sure, yet. Sasha? Please find out what you can about students turning to sex work to fund their courses. Come on, let's talk,' she said and Byrd followed Jo into her office.

CHAPTER 28

'Well?' Jo didn't use any pleasantries, more interested in hearing Byrd's news about the two post-mortems.

'Jeremy will be sending over a formal post-mortem report, but in the meantime...' Byrd paused.

Jo grinned, 'For goodness sake, Eddie, spill the beans.'

'John Holt died of excessive strain on the heart.'

'A heart attack? What from?'

'Could have been exertion. Could have been fear. Maybe sex three times in one night with three different girls was just too much for his heart to cope with. I don't know what else to say, really. Jeremy said there doesn't seem to be any strange circumstances surrounding the death.'

'Was there any sign of heart disease?'

'No there wasn't. It could just have been a blip, that didn't self-correct itself, apparently.'

Jo wondered what would have caused a blip in the beating of John Holt's heart. She was beginning to have an inkling, but decided it was best to keep that thought to herself for a while.

'And our dead girl?'

'As we thought, strangulation. Taken in the context of the other two attacks, Jeremy thinks it was an accident, rather than deliberate as there was bruising all over her neck, not just from the fatal squeeze.'

She thanked Byrd and sat at her desk, pulling paperwork towards her. He took the hint and left her office.

Once he'd gone, Jo thought back to last night. Byrd had had a hurried conversation with her. He was trying to come to terms with Jo's gift and had told her that in order to help him understand her and her gifts better he wanted to chat to Keith Thomas and also her father, Mick, if that was okay with her. She'd agreed but Jo wished this was all over. It was like sitting an exam when you didn't know the answers, hell when you didn't even understand the questions. The thing was, it was probably the same for Byrd.

She wasn't sure what Byrd was looking for. Evidence that she was mad? Or evidence that she was sane but was just more tuned-in than most people? The accident and the coma seemed to have triggered something in her brain that had given her this gift. Awakened her third eye, or whatever you wanted to call it. But the waiting was getting to her. At work he was fine with her, but cooler. More formal. There were no shared secrets anymore. No lingering touches or looks, no evenings to look forward to. No weekends

Oh for goodness sake, pull yourself together, she admonished herself. Since when had life really been a bed of roses. Take off those tinted glasses.

Sasha wandered in, without knocking or asking permission and handed Jo copies of newspaper reports. 'They're about sex work and students,' she said.

'Oh, thanks, Sasha,' said Jo. No longer did Jo bother to admonish Sasha for her strange behaviour, in favour of accepting the woman for who and what she was. 'Have you copies for the others?'

Sasha nodded.

'Great, hand them out then, would you?'

Once more Sasha mutely nodded and left Jo's office. On the copies there were no details of what newspapers the quotes or reports had come from, nor any dates. But to be honest it didn't really matter. For now they just wanted information. Jo turned back to the first page and began reading:

During a fitness-to-study meeting, university staff said they were going to take disciplinary action against one of their students because she was bringing the university into "moral disrepute".

She said: 'I was very open with them about the sex work in the meeting. It was quite striking that the meeting was set up to help me – and then I was being met with punishment at the end.

'I thought, you want me to escape sex work but then in order to punish me for doing sex work you are going to remove the only opportunity I have, my degree, to escape it,..' was the girl's response.

And she is not alone. 'The ECP have fought a number of cases recently where universities have threatened to throw out students if they do not stop doing sex work,' Ms Watson said.'

The University of Brighton launched an investigation at the start of the academic year after its student union faced heavy criticism for allowing a sex worker outreach stall at their freshers' fair.

Critics suggested that the presence of the support group – which also had a stall at the University of Sussex – was advocating and encouraging sex work among students.

Collating official figures on the number of sex workers is difficult because many are worried they will face negative consequences by becoming more visible.

But figures from money advice website Save the Student this year found more than one in 10 students use their bodies – including sex work, sugar daddy dating and webcamming – to make money.

Sugar daddying, where younger women are paid to go on dates often with older men, is becoming increasingly popular, data suggests. Last year, sugar daddy website Seeking Arrangement saw hundreds more subscriptions from university students.

The rise of technology has meant webcamming has also become a more attractive option to students due to its flexibility and ease – and because there are less risks than face-to-face work.

Another student at a university in Wales, who did not wish to be named, said she would not have considered sex work if it had not been online.

'I have an anxiety disorder, and meeting new people is quite a stressful thing for me. Face-to-face doesn't appeal to me at all,' she said.

The 23-year-old, who started making sex videos in her second year, said her friends were not surprised when she told them about her work. 'It is probably becoming more normal because it is more accessible with the internet,' she said.

The student makes around £70 a week for recording videos, and the money pays for her food and petrol.

She said: 'I would like to think there is less of a stigma among students because most students probably know someone who does it. I think more people are choosing it.' But there is still a lack of support for students who do sex work. 'It doesn't get spoken about,' she said. 'It would be nice to have a support network within the university.'

The National Union of Students (NUS), as well as some student unions (SUs) and societies, have tried to raise awareness and support sex workers to reduce the discrimination they face.

But very few universities signpost support networks for sex workers on their websites. And some SU officers who asked for resources were blocked by the institutions, according to ECP.

'Universities are worried about the bad press,' Ms Watson said. 'They are relying on good press and people's money coming in.'

A student sex worker in the southwest of England told The Independent: 'Most universities have a tendency to deny that students are sex workers.' She added, 'The first step would be to address it. Only from acknowledgement would be a realisation that this is something that is happening and something we need to tackle. Universities have a duty to their students to provide support regardless of the backlash.'

Sarah Lasoye, women's officer for the NUS, said: 'Universities as a whole need to take a much less judgemental outlook on the types of work that students are doing. Their priority should be making sure these students are safe and healthy', she added.

Jo put the papers down. So that's why the three girls had

turned to sex work. Money. Pure and simple. Desperate for a university degree but equally desperate to avoid the money trap that three or four years at Uni could become. Money-savvy students were turning to selling sex, in one form or another.

It was possible that someone had been 'watching' the girls and had chosen them specifically. They were young, mostly drug and alcohol free, better mother material than the older women, or the obviously under age girls, who also patrolled the streets.

Judging from the messages left by the Pumpkin Man and the refusal of him to wear a condom, Jo figured it was a safe bet that he was hoping that the girls would become pregnant.

CHAPTER 29

Byrd was still having problems adjusting to Jo's new normal and that was something he'd have to face up to. Sometimes he thought it was the 'gift' and at others he was sure it was because she'd kept it from him for so long. Didn't she trust him with her secret? Didn't she think she could rely on him, or lean on him? As a result he was sure of one thing. She didn't feel about him the same way that he felt about her. And he wasn't sure how to get past that.

At her suggestion, he'd agreed to meet with Keith Thomas, her contact at the Spiritualist Church, but he hadn't arranged anything yet. Again, he was aware that he was prevaricating, trying everything he could to not turn and face the problem. He'd backed himself into a corner and didn't know what the next sensible move would be. He sighed as his desk phone rang. He really didn't want any interruptions. He'd been tasked with locating any CCTV footage they could find of the three incidents. Jill and Ken were concentrating on Storm and Suki and Byrd was dealing with the dead girl's murder.

He answered his phone with an abrupt, 'DS Byrd.'

'Hi Eddie,'

Byrd sat upright from the slouching position he'd adopted as he stared at his monitor.

'Oh, hi, Mick. Did you want Jo?' Byrd said, thinking that the call had been put onto the wrong phone.

'No, I wanted a chat with you, actually.'

'Really?' Eddie was instantly on his guard.

'Yes, um fancy and pie and a pint?' Byrd grinned. Mick hadn't changed at all.

'Sure thing, but I'll have an alcohol-free pint. I'm on duty.'

'Oh, sorry, yes, of course.'

'What time?' Byrd looked at his watch, it was 12.30 pm.

'Um, now? I'm outside?'

'Of course you are, Mick. Yes, give me a couple of minutes.'

'Great. See you in a bit.'

Byrd replaced the receiver. He wondered what Mick wanted, but if he were a betting man, he would say it was about Jo.

Byrd popped his head around Jo's office door. 'Just off for a lunch break, Boss.'

Jo nodded. 'Thanks, Byrd.'

He could feel her eyes on him as he left the floor. Before Odin, they'd have tried to lunch together, if they got a break at all. Now, post Odin, he did his own thing and didn't tell her where he was going or if he was meeting anyone. And if he was, who he was meeting and why.

A petty dig, maybe, but a way of keeping himself separate. On his own, rather than part of a couple. The trouble was, if he was honest with himself, the whole thing just made him feel lonely and alone.

As Byrd walked out of the police station, he saw Mick across the road, waiting for him.

Shaking hands in greeting, Mick led the way to his chosen pub. Byrd wasn't very hungry but readily agreed to lunch. Somehow the process of choosing something to eat, then actually eating it, would lighten the intense conversation they would no doubt have.

Taken up with that, Byrd didn't take much notice of a man sat at their table. The pub was crowded so it made sense to share. It wasn't until Mick introduced the man as Keith Thomas from the local Spiritualist church, that the penny dropped.

'Mick...' Eddie warned.

'Look, Eddie, this was the quickest way to get you to hear us out. If I'd have phoned suggesting a longer meeting, with myself and Mr Thomas here, then you'd have declined the invitation. Am I right?'

'Too right,' Eddie confirmed.

'So as you're already here, and you've just ordered some lunch, why don't we have a conversation?'

'Oh, go on.'

Mick grinned. 'Thanks, Eddie. I'll let Keith introduce himself.'

Keith Thomas looked nothing like a pastor or priest. He didn't wear a clerical collar. He had sandy blond hair that fell straight over his forehead. He was wearing a checked shirt with a v-neck jumper over it and no tie. Very normal. Very non-threatening.

'Hi, Eddie. Can I call you Eddie?'

'Of course, Eddie or Byrd, I answer to either.'

'It might be best if I tell you upfront that neither Mick nor Jo attend our Spiritualist Church. They don't treat Jo's gift as a religious experience. In fact their attitude is refreshing. They remain open to possibilities without getting stuck in the dogma.'

'So?'

'So, the church exists to promote spiritualism, to provide a meeting place where people can come together in peace and love and provide an opportunity to search and discover spiritual truth. Through spiritual communication we hope to provide evidence of survival of the human spirit after the physical death. We do not profess to provide proof. And I feel that's vitally important, especially in Jo's case. For you, witnessing a demonstration of Jo's mediumship should be viewed as an opportunity to gather your own evidence; it is for you to decide whether the evidence is substantial. Obviously, in time, the three of us hope you will gather sufficient evidence to swing the balance of your opinion to accept the concept of survival of the spirit.'

Keith fell silent and took a drink from his pint glass. 'And that's it?' Byrd was confused.

'Yes. In essence, that's it.'

'None of us want to pressurise you into anything, Byrd. We're not trying to brainwash you.'

Eddie coloured at that one, because to an extent he'd thought Mick and Jo were.

'You've seen with your own eyes what the spirits can achieve. You either believe that and trust what your eyes saw, or you don't. But if you decide you're not convinced, then that's fine. But why should that interfere with your relationship with Jo?'

Eddie drank from his own drink, mostly to give him time to reflect on his answer. He was also grateful that the food arrived at the same time as well. By the time they'd sorted out knives and forks and condiments, he was ready to answer.

'Put like that, well no.'

'No?'

'No it shouldn't interfere with my relationship with Jo.'

Mick nodded, but it was Keith who spoke up. 'Think of it as one person being Catholic and the other person being Protestant. Or even Jewish and Muslim. How about one black and the other white. Take your pick.'

Eddie cut into his food and chewed on it thoughtfully. 'So looking at our differences from that point of view, they begin to be less restrictive.'

'Absolutely,' agreed Mick. 'You can believe her, or not. The question is more do you believe IN her? As a woman, as a partner, or even as your boss.'

Byrd felt affronted. 'Of course I believe IN her, as you put it.'

'Then maybe it's about time you started to show it. Another drink anyone?'

Eddie shook his head and putting his knife and fork to one side, said, 'I need some air. Nice to meet you, Keith. See you, Mick,' and he elbowed his way out of the crowded pub. It was becoming claustrophobic, what with the many patrons and the pressure he'd felt from Mick and Keith.

Once outside he was grateful for the fresh air and leaned against the wall dragging oxygen into his lungs, hoping that would stop his trembling legs. Wanting to get the taste of alcohol-free lager out of his mouth he queued up at a local take away for a coffee. Once he had that, he wandered over to a free bench and sat looking at the Cathedral. In the city centre you couldn't get away from the structure. It dominated the skyline. But did it have much effect on the local people? He wasn't sure that it did. It had never meant much to Byrd himself; it had just always been there. There were others in the community who lived their lives in the shadow of the cathedral. Embraced it. Volunteered. Had faith, had belief. So carrying on that analogy Jo's gift will always be there, dominating her. But she used her gift for good. He understood that. How did she put it? Oh yes, 'to help solve the crimes of the living with the aid of the dead'.

Given that, why should Byrd have a problem with it? It was her belief, her practice, her gift. Not his. Jo wasn't asking for validation of her gift, but validation of HER. He was beginning to realise that he had done her a grave disservice. By refusing to accept her for who she was, he was turning his back on her love, her goodness, her kindness. She was a bloody good police officer with or without her gift. She was committed to her team, her family, her life. She was more alive than anyone he knew. And without her, he felt dead.

CHAPTER 30

Just as Byrd was about to leave the gardens, Mick came hurrying along. 'Glad I caught you, Byrd, can I just have five minutes?'

Not feeling that he had much of an option, Byrd nodded and sat back down on the bench.

Mick huffed as he joined him. 'Look, Byrd, I might be speaking out of turn, but I can't not speak up. You understand?'

Byrd nodded.

'You know what Jo went through to get back to full health. No one is more determined than my Jo.'

'I know that, Mick.'

'Well, then you'll know that she is determined to use her gift in the best way that she can.'

'Which is?'

'To help people! For God's sake, Byrd, are you so blind that you can't see that it's still Jo underneath all this? Just because you now know about her extra capabilities, it doesn't make her anything less. She's still the person you fell in love with.'

Byrd looked sideways at Mick. He had never articulated his feelings about Jo to anyone, not even to himself if he was honest.

'Oh for goodness sake, man, I've seen the way you are around her, the looks you give her when you think no one is looking. Why are you refusing to let yourself be happy? Why are you refusing to see her gift as a positive thing? But if you choose Jo, then you choose to believe in her and just maybe believe in her gift. From what I hear you've seen evidence of it.'

'Yes, I suppose, that debacle with Odin.' Byrd had to admit, albeit grudgingly. He looked down and kicked at the ground. Byrd was beginning to feel like a teenager being told off by a parent.

'And it worked didn't it?' persisted Mick. 'It banished Odin?'

'Well he certainly hasn't ever been found. And the BNL have faded away as well.'

'Look, Byrd, it's up to you, but I hear Judith's been sitting at your shoulder too.'

'What? Judith's dead.'

'Of course she is, but she visits Jo and now you.'

'Well...' Byrd refused to be drawn into that conversation.

'That's what I thought. Look, to be harsh, you've got to make a decision. You can't keep this 'on the bus' and 'off the bus' stuff going any longer. You need to commit, one way or the other. It's not fair on Jo otherwise, keeping her hanging, hoping. If you prevaricate much longer, she'll throw you under the sodding bus herself,' and Mick grinned.

Byrd gave him a long searching look. 'You're right. I need to make things right with Jo. Thanks, Mick,' and Byrd stood and shook Mick's hand.

As Byrd left, he still didn't know what his decision was, but he guessed he'd better make his mind up sooner rather than later. Talk about being under the microscope, but the only way to stop it was to do something about it.

Mick was not the only person watching Byrd walk away. Harry Sykes had been walking past the gardens, when he saw the striking figure of Mick Walsh. The man had always had a presence about him, barrel chested and muscular, yet nimble of foot. Wondering what had taken place between the two men, Sykes thought he might as well try and find out.

'Mick!' he called and raised an arm.

Looking around, Mick saw him and raised his hand in greeting. Sykes wasn't sure if he'd receive a warm reception but decided to chance it. As the two men met and shook hands, Mick said, 'I'd heard a rumour you'd moved to Chichester. How are you finding it?'

'Oh, you know, still finding my feet. And you? How's retirement?'

'Never knew I'd be so busy,' laughed Mick. But Sykes detected a note of forced merriment. Or was that just envy on his part?

'How's Jo?' Sykes asked.

'I'd have thought you'd know that better than me,' Mick's eyes narrowed. 'Or don't you take much notice of your DI's?'

'Of course, I just meant personally.'

'Then I suggest you ask her,' said Mick. 'Sorry, must be off,' and he turned on his heel and left Sykes feeling affronted.

Sykes wondered what had made Mick so prickly. Granted they hadn't been friends exactly all those years ago, but Mick seemed to think Sykes was fishing. Maybe he was. He wondered if Mick and Jo had something to hide. He guessed time would tell and walked off to buy himself some lunch. But if he caught a whiff of anything untoward, well he'd make it his business to find out what they were hiding.

As soon as Sykes walked off, Mick turned to watch him. He'd never liked Sykes when they were on the task force together. There was just something 'off' with him. Mick always felt Sykes made his flesh creep. He was just so cold. Had no empathy for victims or their families. He was abrupt to the point of rudeness and had those dead eyes that Mick had seen in the worst of humanity - sociopaths, and psychopaths. Not that Mick was saying that's what Sykes was, he just had the same detached attitude as them. He'd come across colleagues who had known Sykes over the years, and it seemed he'd climbed the ladder on the backs of others. Taking credit for other's work. Pushing himself forward, ingratiating himself with senior officers. He certainly knew how to play the game; Mick gave him that. He worried for Jo working under him, but according to her she didn't have much to do with him. But Mick knew that if she failed to find any evidence, or produce credible suspects in a case, she would be roundly criticised. Sykes himself would never take the blame, never accept criticism of his leadership, it would always be someone else's fault.

He'd have to keep an eye on Jo, but for now he'd keep his opinions to himself.

CHAPTER 31

That evening, Jo arrived home exhausted. Not really from the case, but from staying positive, happy and acting as though there was nothing wrong. She dumped her bag, shoes and coat and headed straight for the shower.

As the hot needles of spray touched her skin and massaged her back and shoulders, she began to relax. She decided to wash her hair while she was there. It was still short and messy as she'd rather grown to like the style. After Anubis hacked at it, a hairdresser in town had managed to salvage something from it and now Jo kept it short, which was much more manageable than before.

Turning off the water and then wrapping herself in towels, she cleared the mist from the mirror on the bathroom cabinet. She yelped as instead of her face staring back at her, she was looking at Judith.

'Stop with the mirrors, Judith, you keep scaring the shit out of me!'

'Sorry, it's easier for me to appear in mirrors. Anyway to business, you do realise that John Holt is not the real perpetrator, not the person behind the rapes, although he would have found it hard to persuade anyone that that was the case.'

'That's my impression. I saw something when I had a vision from Storm. A black being hovering over John Holt. She also said John seemed to change during the act of sex.'

'I also think Holt was killed to stop him talking.'

Jo nodded her agreement. 'So do we. But how literally do we take this fallen angels procreating with humans?'

Judith appeared to think for a moment, before starting, 'Biblical stories are often fantastical, unbelievable and sometimes confusing when it comes to interpreting their meaning. Of the apocryphal biblical texts, I understand there are few more enigmatic and fascinating than the Book of Enoch.'

'Do some believe that, Judith? Beings from outer space?'

'To be honest I'm not sure, but I'll tell you things have happened this year that I'd never imagined in heaven or earth. I'm not the font of all knowledge, Jo, I can't answer your questions about the Book of Enoch. Has the curate shed any light on it?'

'Not that I'm aware, but Jill is liaising with him.'

'Oh, is that what you call it these days?'

'What? OMG No! Really? I thought she looked a bit doe eyed at him.'

'Looks that way. At the very least she's developing rather an interest in all things Cathedral.'

'And on that happy note I'm going to get dressed and dry my hair before I catch my death.'

As Jo went to get dressed, she wished her young DC well. Everyone in this game needed someone to lean on every now and again. At least if she lost Eddie, she'd always have Mick.

CHAPTER 32

The Watcher moved among the shadows of the night. Along the lanes and alleyways, where he merged into the darkness, flitting here and there. All the time attuned to the small changes in the forces protecting his son. He would stay close. Guarding him. Watching over him. He was confident that Edith would look after Damien. A rather fitting name. A stroke of genius from Edith. He would continue watching over him for the first few months of his life, leave him with his mother. Then strike. Take him. For a son needed his father.

John Holt was gone and the police were focused on his death, trying to find his killer. But they would never find him. The Watcher left behind no clues. Nothing of himself. And anyway they couldn't actually find him and arrest him, for to all intents and purposes he didn't exist. For after all he wasn't human. He could come and go as he pleased, and they would see nothing but shadows. Feel nothing but a slight change in the air as he passed. Teasing. Frightening. Invisible.

Holt was nothing but a patsy. A stupid man who had

been bought for a few measly pounds. It never ceased to amaze him how stupid some humans were. Blinded by sex, money, or violence. Whatever it took to buy their co-operation. And usually it didn't take very much at all. Holt had deserved all he got. Which in the end, of course, was nothing.

Halloween had been a good night's work for all that. Two out of the three women pregnant. Shame about the woman that died. Not that her death meant anything to him per se. It was just that she represented a lost chance for another child. Still mustn't be greedy, he thought.

As the first few fingers of dawn broke through the shadows, he returned to his place atop the Cathedral, settling on his perch, becoming one with the stone. Just another gargoyle, one amongst many. Watching over the city that had become his own.

Abbey mumbled in her sleep and turned over, her arm reaching for the cot and her baby, before falling back on the bed as she relaxed once more. Her blond hair spread over the pillow was damp at the roots and her eyes under the closed lids jumped this way and that. Her body, clad in pyjamas, had slimmed down after the birth of Damien. Her skin, having the elasticity of youth, had contracted over her stomach, only leaving a few faint stretch marks.

Her dream was becoming more of a nightmare. In it she fought off those who would take her son from her. Invisible beings with evil in their souls. But she fought like the devil himself to keep her son safe. For the first time in her life she was responsible for someone other than herself. She recognised that finally she had grown up. Her baby deserved the best from his mother, and she was ready to take up that challenge.

CHAPTER 33

By the middle of January, after the Christmas celebrations were over, when all looked cold and frozen from the wind blowing in from the sea, Jo was finding it hard to be positive. She was disappointed in the team's progress with the recent rapes and murders, or rather lack of it. The problem was that only Jo seemed to think that someone, or something, had killed John Holt. Everyone else was happy with the heart attack from natural causes theory. She was about to have a meeting with Sykes about her cases and wasn't looking forward to it.

She entered his office with some trepidation. Jo still didn't feel that comfortable with the new DCI even though it had been a while since he'd joined them. He kept himself apart, watching over his teams rather than interacting with them. He was so different from Alex, although Jo realised, she had to stop comparing them. Maybe that was why she hadn't warmed to their new boss, she still hankered after the old one. But Sykes did nothing to make the teams like him. It wasn't just Jo, other DI's felt the same way as she did. He was a bit of a queer fish most thought. Maybe the line that he wanted to move south for weather and the beaches was just a load of bullshit. Perhaps he was told to leave Manchester and had been relocated somewhere else. No one in Chichester had any contacts in the Greater Manchester police force, so if there were any rumours surrounding his transfer, they hadn't heard any.

Sykes got straight to it and wanted to talk about the rapes last Halloween.

Pulling her mind away from speculations, Jo said to Sykes, 'Storm and Suki both know that Holt is dead and will never bother them again. They'll never stumble across him, never have to confront the man that violated them. He is gone, never to return.'

'Ah, but is he the rapist?'

'Well,' Jo started carefully, 'All the forensic testing has come back, the inquest open and closed and both Storm and Suki identified John Holt as their attacker.'

'Remind me about the DNA again?' Sykes sat back in his chair and regarded Jo with shrewd eyes. Another habit that felt to Jo as though he was keeping himself separate. Backing away from close physical contact with anyone.

'Holt's DNA didn't match the DNA found in the semen taken from the three victims.'

'That's how I remembered it. So was he really our man?' The unspoken criticism that Jo had identified the wrong suspect hung in the air.

'I admit we've still not managed a match with any DNA in our databanks.

'Which meant we can't formally confirm that Holt had been the rapist and murderer. One of the girls didn't make it, remember.'

There it was. Out in the open. But Jo wasn't finished.

'On the other hand both Suki and Storm had his skin cells under their fingernails and hairs from his head and pubic hairs were lifted from their bodies. They also said they rang 999 straight after he attacked them.

'Maybe they were confused?'

'I beg your pardon?'

'Perhaps they had another client after him but because of the attack had got confused as to who did what.'

'There's never been an indication of that, Sir.' Jo was adamant.

'But you have to admit it is a possibility.'

'Well, yes, but…'

Sykes cut her off. 'In that case, there's still a murdering rapist out there somewhere and you haven't caught him yet.' Sykes was silent for a moment. Then he sat up in his chair and closed the file on his desk. 'You can't close the case. Keep trying to match the DNA. We need a result on this one, Jo.'

'Yes, Sir,' She knew this case was turning out to be a black mark against her and she felt that Sykes wouldn't hesitate to throw her to the wolves if he got the chance. She was getting a bit fed up with the constant criticism. A bit of praise now and then wouldn't go amiss.

CHAPTER 34

Jo and Byrd had spoken little on the short drive to where Suki still lived. She thought he looked tired. There were dark smudges under his eyes and he hadn't shaved that morning. As they got out of the car, she teased, 'Ran out of time this morning, did you? Or is this the new Byrd?'

'Sorry?'

'Just wondered if you were aiming for designer stubble.'

Byrd smiled. 'Ah this,' he said as his hand rasped over his chin. 'Ran out of time to shave this morning, that's all. Why? Do you like it?'

'Mmm,' said Jo. 'Not sure that it's an improvement.'

She was stopped from saying anything else, as Suki opened the door at Byrd's knock.

'Hey, Suki, how are you?' Byrd said. 'We'd like a chat with you if that's alright?'

'Oh right, come in then.'

They were shown into a messy, but homely living room with plenty of evidence of the student inhabitants. Magazines and newspapers were strewn around, the tv was on with the sound turned down, so the super shiny couple on the morning programme were reduced to a background babble. Suki collected mugs and plates in an attempt to tidy up.

'Please sit down so we can talk,' said Jo.

'No, let me get rid of these first.'

Jo and Byrd nodded. Jo figured Suki needed time to pull herself together after the shock of seeing them on her doorstep.

'What's this all about?' said Suki coming back into the room. 'Only I don't know that I can face another discussion about the case. To be honest I'm not feeling the best at the moment, not since I lost the baby.'

'Baby?' Echoed Jo.

'Lost it?' asked Byrd.

'Oh, didn't you know? The bastard got me pregnant. I was trying to decide what to do when I had a miscarriage. It was awful, the worst thing ever. But it's over now and I'm trying to come to terms with the whole bloody thing. Oh and I've given up sex work as well. I guess I'd rather be poor. Anyway what did you want?'

'Please sit, Suki,' said Jo gently. They all found spaces to sit and Jo continued. 'We're here to ask you if you're sure that John Holt was your rapist? Is it possible that there was another client after John and you'd confused the two?'

Suki looked at them, with tears building in her eyes. 'You don't believe me,' she said.

'Oh, Suki, of course we do. But we need to ask you. Are you sure John Holt was your rapist?'

'Positive. No question. Why are you asking me? Don't you believe me? Do you think I'm lying?' Suki was shouting and crying, and tears were tracking down her cheeks.

'No, no, sorry, of course not.'

'What is the matter with you people? I suffered horrendously at the hands of that... that... bastard!'

Jo handed Suki a tissue from her pocket. 'Here,' she said, 'dry your eyes.'

Suki took the tissue but didn't wipe her eyes, instead she said, 'I'm sticking with my story, it was John Holt that attacked me, but he changed during the act. Became someone or something else. Afterwards I couldn't get away from that 'thing'. He wouldn't leave me alone. I felt like I was being watched all the time, no matter where I went in town or at Uni.'

'And now?'

'Since I lost the baby, nothing. He's gone. And all I want now is to be left alone.' Suki finally dried her eyes and stood. 'And that includes by you two. So I suggest you go and harass someone else.'

CHAPTER 35

After Jo and Byrd had climbed in the car, he turned to her. 'What did Suki mean? About being watched?'

'You know what she meant, Byrd.' Jo ran her hand through her hair. 'You know as well as I do.'

He shook his head. 'No. No. No!' He banged his fist on the steering wheel

She took his hand and was relieved when he didn't pull away. 'Yes! Look Suki said as much when we first found her. That John Holt changed somehow. Became something else. And ever since then that 'being' was watching her. Dad says you've talked to him and to Keith. You've seen Judith. Hell, you were watching when we confronted Odin. So don't ask what she meant. You already know the answer to the question. Now let's go and see Storm.'

Byrd shook his head, but started the car, nevertheless.

It was only a short ride to Storm's flat. They still hadn't spoken when Storm opened the door at Jo's knock.

Once inside, Storm stood and looked at them. 'Well?'

The question was a challenge as well as a query and Storm crossed her arms across her chest. She was wearing jeans and a tee-shirt, her bare foot tapping on the rather dirty carpet. Jo was glad she had shoes on. Who knew what was hiding in the fibres? Still, it took her back to her own student days.

Pulling her attention back to Storm, she said, 'We just wanted to see if you were okay.'

'And?'

'And what?'

'This isn't a social call, that's not what you people do. So why are you really here?'

Jo could feel the anger emanating from Storm, who appeared to be living up to her name. 'Why don't you sit down so we can talk.'

'No. You're not staying.'

Jo sighed. 'Very well, we just wanted to clarify if you are sure that John Holt was your rapist?'

'Of course he was, you had the evidence to prove it!'

'Yes, I know, but is it possible that there was a client after John and before you called the police?' Jo wished Byrd would join in the conversation, but he remained implacable. He seemed as angry as Storm; he just wasn't vocalising it. But she could see the muscle in his jaw ticking. 'Perhaps because of the attack you became confused?'

'You really believe that? All I know is that John Holt raped me because he turned into something or someone else. I've been watched ever since the rape. That prickling at the back of the neck as though you've been stung by nettles.' Storm was calming down, her anger burnt out. 'It was worse around the Cathedral. That was really freaky. I always felt someone watching me around there. As though they were above me, you know?

Looking down. But the only thing up there is gargoyles. They really freaked me out. I could have sworn one of them was following me with his eyes.'

'A gargoyle?' Jo wasn't liking the sound of this.

'Yeah, bloody horrible creepy things they are. Anyway, as I was saying, after the abortion, nothing, gone. He, it, has left me alone ever since, thank goodness. And I intend to keep it that way.'

'Abortion?'

Storm nodded. 'I told you he refused to wear a condom. That was my worst nightmare. Getting pregnant. You know? Anyway it won't happen again.'

'Are you giving up the work?'

Storm nodded. 'I've gone virtual.'

Jo smiled.

'All it took was one video of me being provocative and pretending to masturbate, which they sell over and over again and I get commission every time it's watched. Not bad, eh?'

Jo grinned, 'And safer too.'

'Yes, much.'

CHAPTER 36

Abbey had finished her new design at last. She sighed with relief as she put down her sketch pad. The dress was for a particularly demanding client who was going to a fancy-dress party and probably had more money than sense. She had a clear idea of what she wanted, rather than what Abbey thought she should have. Abbey wasn't happy about that way of working, but to be honest she needed the money. She'd scan the designs later and send them over so the woman could choose which one she wanted.

She stood and stretched and patted her flabby tummy, which was nearly back to normal. It was just that the last few pounds were proving harder to get rid of than she'd imagined. But she didn't mind, it was a reminder of her beautiful baby, Damien. Thinking of Damien, where was he? She looked at her watch. Edith had taken him for a walk over 2 hours ago now. Abbey had been so engrossed in her work that she hadn't noticed the time. Prickles of alarm ran down her spine. Then she admonished herself for being stupid. Edith was a wonderful friend. Damien would be safe with her. Wouldn't he?

Abbey grabbed her mobile and rang Edith's number. Unobtainable. No such number. Abbey looked at her phone as though she didn't recognise it. It wasn't possible. Surely she must have misdialled. Perhaps rung someone else by mistake. But there were no other 'E's' in her contact list. Nevertheless she tried Edith's number again. And got the same message. Unobtainable. No such number.

She paced the room and tried to remember what Edith had said. Something about taking him for a walk to the park to feed the ducks. That was it! Grabbing her coat she left the house and ran all the way to the park. Gasping for breath she rushed to the duck pond. Nothing. No Damien. No Edith. In fact there was no one there at all. She jogged all around the park, calling for Damien and for Edith, but her only reply was the cawing of birds hiding in the trees.

Calm down, she admonished herself. Think. Had Edith said anything else? She felt as though the park was spinning around her head, like some sort of slide show. Going faster and faster. Abbey gasped for breath but couldn't get any oxygen into her lungs. The park spun faster. Abbey began to scream until there was nothing left inside her, and she collapsed on the grass.

She came round to see a worried face looking down at her. 'Are you alright?' the woman said. 'Can you get up? What's happened?'

Abbey sat up, put head between her knees, taking deep breaths. The woman stayed beside her, but didn't touch her. Didn't hold out a helping hand, so Abbey struggled to her feet under her own steam. She swayed slightly, then the park came back into sharp focus and she remembered. 'Damien,' she gasped. 'Have you seen an elderly woman with a baby in a pram?' She reached out to grab the woman's coat but it seemed to slip through her fingers and she couldn't get a purchase on it.

'No sorry.'

Abbey couldn't see anyone else in the park. Her and the woman were the only two people. 'Who are you?'.

'Oh, sorry, my name is Judith.'

Abbey nodded but the name didn't mean anything to her. She didn't know a Judith. Had never actually met one. Who was she and why was she there? Had she had something to do with her child? She felt fear curdling in her stomach. 'My friend took the baby out for a walk and she hasn't come back. Are you sure you haven't seen her?'

'No, I'm sorry I can't help. Maybe you've missed her and she's waiting for you at home.' Judith raised her hand and gave Abbey the lightest push.

'Oh, God, you're right. I should never have left the house,' and Abbey sprinted off. Realising she hadn't thanked Judith, she looked behind her, but there was no one there. Abbey thought that strange and then for a brief moment Judith came back into view, but it was a different Judith. One that looked as though the whole of her back had been burned. And her hair was a frizzy mess. Abbey hadn't noticed that before.

Who the hell was she?

But that was a question for another time Abbey thought and put all her effort into getting back home as quickly as she could.

CHAPTER 37

Storm had just closed the door behind them when Jo's phone rang. Annoyed, because she'd wanted to speak to Byrd, she spat, 'Yes?'

'Boss, it's Jill. We've a missing child. Sykes said we are to take the case. I've told Bill and uniform are on their way. I'm sending you a text with the address. Young mother, single parent, name of Abbey.'

'Thanks, Jill. You and Ken meet us there. Is Sykes on his way?

'No,' said Jill. 'He said his presence wasn't necessary.'

Sykes was definitely a 'hands off' and not a 'hands on' boss. She cut the call and told Byrd. They'd not had a chance to speak about Byrd's denial of all things supernatural and now that conversation would be shoved to the back of the queue. Again. Oh well. There were more important things than their tiffs. Far more important. And a child in danger was at the top of that list.

Byrd drove as Jo read out the address and they pulled up to find marked police cars and an ambulance already at the scene. Tape was in place, Bill and his team were getting ready to go into the house and the mother was sat on the steps of the ambulance wrapped in a blanket. Her teeth were chattering and she pulled the blanket tighter around her shoulders.

'How is she?' Jo asked Bill.

'When uniforms arrived, she was hysterical, unable to stop sobbing. She confessed she'd fainted in the park when she couldn't find her boy and I gather she still feels faint. That's why there's an ambulance here, everyone was very concerned about her.'

'Thanks, Bill.'

Now she had a little information, Jo sat one step down from Abbey at the back of the ambulance. 'Hi,' she said. 'My name is Jo and I'm a police officer. I'm going to do everything I can to find your baby. Now, can you tell me what happened?'

'Um, yes,' Abbey hesitated as her voice broke on just those two words. She cleared her throat and tried again. 'It was just a normal morning. I was working, the baby had been asleep when Edith came over. She took Damien for a walk and they never came back.'

'So the last person you saw was this Edith?'

Abbey nodded. 'She went out to give Damien some fresh air and to give me a break and hasn't been seen since. What am I to do? Where is my baby? What's happened to Edith? I can't believe she would have done anything to harm Damien.'

'Has anyone been in touch with you since then? Phone calls, visitors, anything?'

'Just that piece of paper shoved under my door.'

It took all Jo's restraint to keep the excitement out of her voice and ask calmly, 'What did it say? Do you still have it?'

'It was quite long, a load of rubbish if you ask me, but I gave it to that bloke over there,' and Abbey pointed to Bill. 'The one with the funny suit on.'

'Perfect, Abbey,' said Jo. 'Well done. Now just hang on and I'll be right back. Oh look, here's Jill, she can sit with you for a while,' and Jo motioned Jill over. 'I'm just going to see Bill about a note pushed under Abbey's door,' she whispered. 'Stay with her.'

Jill Sandy nodded and took Jo's place on the steps.

Jo and Byrd rushed over to Bill.

'We hear there's a note?' said Byrd.

Bill nodded. 'Here,' and he handed Byrd a piece of paper in a clear plastic evidence envelope.

Byrd read out loud: And they became pregnant, and they had great giants, whose height was three thousand ells: Who consumed all the acquisitions of men. And when men could no longer sustain them, the giants turned against them and devoured mankind.'

Jo and Byrd looked at each other and said, 'Osian Price.'

As they entered the Cathedral, they heard the music soaring through the huge building, A volunteer helper directed them to the organ.

'We've got to interrupt him,' said Jo. 'We can't possibly wait until he's finished.'

'Hang on,' Byrd said and climbed the stairs.

Jo was left alone and shivered. The Cathedral seemed huge, but not welcoming, rather cold and implacable. Maybe it was just the vestiges of how she felt in the gardens when they were looking for Osian. She'd looked up at the gargoyles and remembered Storm's warning that the gargoyles were menacing, and she'd felt eyes following her. That was just how Jo had felt and she hadn't recovered from it yet. She still had goose bumps on her arms.

Moments later the music came to a crashing halt, then Osian and Byrd appeared.

'Is there a quiet spot where we can talk?' Jo was very aware of tourists and residents and they needed to have a very private conversation. Osian led them through a maze of rooms to the clergy offices. They entered an empty room and Jo showed him the latest message.

'A young child has been snatched and this was left behind. What the hell does it mean, Osian?'

'What's the mothers name?'

'Abbey... Sorry can't remember her surname. Why? Does the name mean something?'

Osian groped behind him for the desk and leaned against it. He'd gone white and his hand was shaking. Osian nodded. A muscle worked in his jaw several times before he managed. 'It means the Watcher has Abbey's child. I think he always was going to take him. He must be his son, a part God, part human child who will be brought up with the Watcher's teachings.'

'You know them? Abbey and her son?'

'Yes, I've kept an eye on her, just from time to time.'

'A lost bird you took under your wing?' Jo guessed.

Osian smiled, 'Yes, you could call it that.'

'Did you notice anything different about the child? Was he like the description in the messages? This one and the previous one?'

'Factually speaking the last description in the list of three messages you showed me, is thought to be of Noah. Others think that's what the hybrid children looked like. So put the two together and some people think Noah was the product of a Watcher. The one thing I noticed was how big the child was. Which would fit with the message left with Abbey.'

'Big?' asked Byrd. 'What exactly are we dealing with here, Osian?'

'Damien is growing faster and faster and he could already be mistaken for a toddler. He is crawling and sitting up and pulling himself up. It's scary what he can do! Abbey knows he is different but can't acknowledge why. She has no recollection of having slept with anyone who could be Damien's father.'

'And you never thought to tell anyone?'

'Who? Why? Should I have come to you and said there's a baby born who could have something to do with the Watchers and the Book of Enoch. Would you even have believed me? What could you have done? Nothing. So no, I didn't say anything. Didn't tell anyone. Tried to forget.'

'It's alright, Osian,' said Jo.

'No it isn't,' Osian said. 'It very much isn't alright. Did you know the child, Damien, was born at 11.55pm on the 31st October?'

Jo thought back to that night. 11.55? Of course, that was it. The feeling she'd had when in the hospital with Storm. A disturbance. Oh crap. This was turning out to be a hell of a day.

One wrong move and they would lose the child forever. It was imperative they find him, and fast. Before the Watcher had a chance to disappear with him.

Osian brough her down to earth with his question, 'What happens now?'

Jo changed gears and instantly became a police officer, not a psychic.

'A snatched child alert is going out and we're going back to see Abbey.' Byrd looked at Jo for confirmation and she nodded her agreement.

'In that case, can I come with you? I will be able to comfort Abbey if nothing else.'

'Of course you can, Osian. Come on, let's go.'

CHAPTER 38

Once back at Abbey's house, Osian joined Jill. Byrd brought out mugs of sweet tea and offered one to the priest, but Osian didn't think he could get anything past the awful blockage in his throat. He was distraught for Abbey but also disgusted with himself for being so afraid. Afraid of speaking out and making a fool of himself. And that fear could have stopped Damien being snatched.

He told Jill of his worries.

'You mustn't think that, Osian,' said Jill. 'If the Watcher was determined to have the child, nothing any of us could have done would have stopped him.'

He approached Abbey, who saw him and stood and clung to him. 'Oh, Osian, someone's got Damien! What will I do without him? You have to help me.'

'We're all here to help, Abbey. Please try not to worry, I'm sure the police know what they're doing.'

'You've been such a good friend, all through the pregnancy and afterward and here you are now when I need someone more than ever.'

'Come on, sit back down, Abbey.' He gently took her

arms to remove her hands from his jacket.

She sat but then stood again, gabbling, looking from Osian to Jill and back again. 'Please help find my baby!' she shouted. Tears shone in her eyes but hadn't yet escaped.

Desperate to calm her, Osian sat on the steps and pulled Abbey down and held her hands. 'Would it help if we prayed.' He hoped it would help for her to focus on something positive instead of her spiralling anxiety.

Abbey nodded. 'I'll do anything, if you think it might do some good.'

Osian thought it might just do him some good, help to ground him. Jill, Osian and Abbey held hands. Osian began, 'Oh Lord we come to ask for your mercy. To ask for you to save Damien, one of your little children. The little children that came to Jesus to be blessed.'

As he continued with the prayers, Osian remembered that Damien hadn't been christened yet, but that was of no matter. For God was surely stronger than the evil Watcher. Just because Damien was spawned of the Devil's seed shouldn't mean that God would turn his back on an innocent child.

After drawing the prayers to a close Osian said, 'Seek peace and solace for yourself, Abbey. Many parents find comfort in their faith and use it as a powerful incentive to survive this nightmare. The loneliness of grief diminishes somewhat for people who believe that they are not alone. Your faith can give you the support and encouragement you need at this critical juncture in your life.'

Abbey nodded and squeezed Osian's hand. Before she could speak, the paramedic wanted her back for a moment to check her vital signs. She was suffering from shock and needed to be kept stable.

Jill and Osian moved away to the front of the vehicle, where they were shielded from the others.

'Hey you,' said Jill. 'Feeling a bit better now?'

He smiled, 'Yes, at least if I'm here I can help if needed. Be a friend to Abbey. Try and calm her down if she hears the worst possible news.' Osian couldn't bring himself to say if they found Damien dead.

'You've been very good to Abbey.'

'Since the first day I saw her I could sense she was like a fledging bird, learning to fly, getting ready to leave the nest. You know she's had a chequered past?'

Jill nodded. 'Drugs and such. She told us. She thought this might be a punishment for all the years of debauchery.'

'Oh, goodness, poor thing. There was always one thing about her though that I never understood until now.'

'Oh?'

'She could never go back into the Cathedral. She only managed it once, the first time we met. After that, it was like she had a panic attack every time she tried. She used to sit outside, she could do that, but never come in.'

'The Watcher,' said Jill.

He nodded. 'Anyway enough talk about me, what about you? Are you okay?'

She smiled. 'Despite today, yes, I'm good.'

'We're good,' and put his arms around her, drawing her into a kiss.

Pulling back, she blushed, 'Osian, not here!'

'Why not here?'

'Because her boss is here,' said another voice.

Jill looked as if she wanted to die on the spot. 'Hi, Boss,' she croaked. 'Um, I was just coming to see you.'

'Really?' Jo arched an eyebrow. 'Osian, Abbey's

asking for you.'

'Oh, yes, of course, thank you,' and he went towards the back of the ambulance trying not to trip over his feet as he inched around Jo.

He heard Jill say, 'Um, Boss, um...'

And Jo's reply, 'It's okay, Jill, but for the moment could you keep your mind on the case and not the curate's assets.'

He smiled at Jo's words. As Abbey was still being worked on by the paramedics he sat on the steps and thought about his relationship with Jill. What kind was it, he asked himself? The thing was he didn't know. Looking to any future that they might have; well he wasn't a Roman Catholic priest where he couldn't marry. They had a lot in common and both had a quirky sense of humour. They were both graduates, and Jill was now studying for a second degree in psychology, in her own time. He didn't know how she fitted it in.

He was of Welsh extraction and they found out that so was she. They weren't intimate yet, for he wouldn't have sex before marriage. But they were becoming closer and closer as the months went by and Jill was attending the Cathedral for the services on a Sunday morning, work permitting. They had a lot in common and all in all he had a good feeling about them and hoped that Jill felt the same way.

He'd decided he didn't want to become a parish priest as he was happiest in the Cathedral environment, which was intellectually stimulating as well as being at the heart of a community. Jill was also wanting to stay in a city environment in her career. She loved the hustle and bustle, the focus on the criminal mind and finding ways to defeat the most hardened criminals. He smiled to himself. Yes, things were going well. Then he immediately felt bad for feeling happy. After all they were there for Abbey, none of this had anything to do with him and Jill. He felt guilty for being happy in the face of poor Abbey's sorrow and banished any romantic thoughts from his mind and turned to Abbey as she was finished with the medic.

'They say I'm OK now,' she told Osian. 'Do you think we can go back inside? After all Damien wasn't snatched from there, was he?'

Osian thought she had a point and said, 'Let's check with DI Wolfe, shall we?'

CHAPTER 39

As Jo walked back towards Abbey's house, Byrd caught up with her.

'I've not had any luck tracing this Edith. I know Abbey gave us a description of her, but with just a first name it's not much to go on. We've checked with the neighbours and Abbey's housemates, but no one remembers seeing anyone looking like that.' He looked at his notebook. 'A girl called Penny who lives with Abbey says she often heard Abbey chatting and thought she must be talking to herself as she worked. Or later on, talking to the baby, like you do. She never saw a visitor.'

Jo frowned. 'And that's it? No one else has seen her?'

'I can't find anyone, Boss, sorry.'

'Right, back to Abbey I think.'

'Abbey,' Jo squatted down to Abbey's level as she was still sitting on the steps of the ambulance. 'We're trying to trace Edith. Do you remember anything about her home life? The people she relied on? Friends? Neighbours?'

'Only the women from the charity shop.'

'Which one?'

'My favourite. The first one you come to as you walk into town. A children's charity, I think.'

'Great, thanks, Abbey. Come on, Byrd.'

'Before you go...'

Jo turned back, 'Yes, Osian?'

'Abbey wondered if she could go back inside.'

'Oh, yes, of course,' Jo replied, and she hurried off. 'Just as quick to walk, I think,' she said to Byrd.

Within a few minutes they were at the shop. It looked bright and welcoming with good quality stock. The window was attractive, with several dresses on mannequins, surrounded by matching shoes and handbags. No wonder Abbey liked this, Jo thought, whoever runs it knows what they're doing.

Pushing through the door, they approached the woman on the desk.

'Good afternoon, I'm DI Jo Walsh and this is DS Eddie Byrd. Can we have a word? In private?'

The police identification appeared to flummox the woman. Her hands fluttered like sparrows, her cheeks reddened, and she silently opened and closed her mouth.

'Perhaps through there?'

The nervous volunteer nodded and followed Jo and Eddie into a stock room. Shelves stacked three sides of the room, filled with every type of clothing imaginable. Coats hung from rails, shoes and boots paired up underneath and in the middle was a large workbench that reminded Jo of the huge areas used by fabric shops and the like. A dry musty smell pervaded the area, reminding Jo of why she disliked charity shops. But for other people they were a mecca, happy to root around for hours for bargains. There were two women working sorting clothes when the three of them entered. Jo introduced herself and Eddie again and asked for their co-operation in the hunt for a missing child.

'We wondered if you had any information on Edith, one of your volunteers.'

It was the younger woman who answered. 'Hi, I'm Liz, the manager. You're looking for Edith? I'm not sure I know anyone by that name. Do you?' she asked the other two women.

They both shook their heads and the nervous woman edged towards the curtain separating the stock room from the shop.

Byrd moved to stop her. 'Are you sure? You don't know her?' he asked.

'No, sorry, I mean yes I am, sure that is. I need to get back outside. Customers, you know?'

He nodded and let the woman pass, who by now was wringing her hands, clearly upset.

Jo frowned at Liz. 'Is she alright?'

Liz nodded. 'Yes, but she suffers from anxiety. Any break in her routine can have her flying into a panic. She's alright. I don't think she's hiding anything if that's what you are worried about.'

Jo considered this, then nodded. The last thing they wanted to do was to upset a vulnerable member of the public.

'You said there's a missing child?'

'Yes, a baby called Damien. His mother, Abbey, said her friend from this shop, Edith, had taken him for a walk and never returned.'

Byrd showed them a picture of Abbey. 'Do you remember this girl?'

'Oh, yes, that's Abbey. She's such a lovely girl. I remember being told she'd had her child. She always used to come in and get clothes and fabrics. I hear she's doing well with her clothes business.'

'But you don't know anyone called Edith?'

The two women shook their heads.

'Elderly lady, retired, steel grey hair, on the small side.' Jo said. She was beginning to get a very bad feeling about this. How could they not know Edith? Abbey said this mysterious woman had helped her a great deal when she'd just started out with her business.

'To be honest that describes most of us,' Liz said, and Jo had to smile at that one. The woman had a point.

'And no one of that name has ever worked here?' Byrd was frowning and Jo could see he was perturbed also.

'No, I've been here five years and I've never had a volunteer called Edith. I'm really sorry.'

'Thanks for your help,' said Jo. 'If you do think of anything that might help us locate this mysterious Edith, please give us a ring,' and Jo handed out her card.

'Of course,' Liz said.

Once outside, Jo and Byrd looked at each other.

'Well that was weird,' he said. 'They've never heard of her? It doesn't make sense.'

'Nothing about this case makes sense,' said Jo. 'Come on, let's get back to Abbey.'

CHAPTER 40

Approaching Abbey, they tried again for any more information about Edith.

'We're so sorry, no one seems to know how to contact her.' Jo thought this was a better approach then telling Abbey the woman who had her baby doesn't seem to exist and they can't find any trace of her. 'Did she ever tell you her surname?'

'You know, come to think of it she didn't.'

'Can you show me a picture of her?'

'Yeah, sure, I think. We snapped some in the park last week,' and she passed her mobile to Jo.

Jo flipped through the pictures but not one of them had an elderly woman with steel grey hair playing with the baby. Jo suppressed her mounting panic, that had started while in the shop. She carefully said, 'Sorry, Abbey, there's none with Edith in.'

'How strange,' said Abbey taking the phone back. 'Maybe they got corrupted or something.'

'Yes, or something,' Jo agreed but kept another possible explanation of the missing photos to herself.

'Shall I draw her?'
'Really? Can you do that?'
'Sure.'
'Thank you for this, Abbey,' said Jo.
'It's okay, it gives me something to focus on, you know?' and once more tears threatened, but she reached for a soft pencil and her sketch book after wiping her eyes.

While Abbey sketched, Jo looked around Abbey's work area. Even though Jo didn't have much interest in clothes, it was easy to see that Abbey was a talented artist and designer from her sketches that were stuck all over the wall. She then thumbed through the items on the rail.

'Abbey, I love these clothes,' said Jo.
'Thanks. But I can't see myself doing any work for a while.'
'Of course not.'
'All I can think about is the baby.'
'Naturally. I take it you have lots of pictures of him.'
'Yes, of course.'
'Can you look through them and send me any recent ones. The more appealing the better.'
'Why? You already have one of him.'
'Yes, but that's for the police officers. I'd like a really cute one of him.'

Abbey nodded. She handed Jo the sketch of Edith and then picked up her phone.

Fairy God Mother, thought Jo as she studied the sketch. Right out of a Disney movie. Too good to be true, she decided, and her heart went out to Abbey. She wondered what Edith really looked like, it was possible Abbey saw what she wanted to see. A close friend taking the place of family. Edith, or whatever her name really was, had clearly seen a need in Abbey and taken full advantage of it.

'I just want to say that we are doing all we can to find Damien. If you hear from anyone about the baby, or even from Edith, let me know immediately. Or let the liaison officer who'll stay with you know. OK?'

'Yes.'

'Promise?' Jo didn't want Abbey to go running off to try and get her baby back on her own.

Abbey nodded. 'Yes, I promise. Oh before you go, Edith took me to hospital in the car, not sure if that helps.'

Jo stilled. 'When?'

'When Damien was born. About three months ago.'

'We might not be able to find CCTV from that far back, but it's certainly worth a shot.'

'Oh, well the midwives saw her.'

'The midwives?'

'Yes, Edith was with me the whole time.'

'And that was on the 31st October.'

'Yes, his date of birth. Oh, he was born late at night, just before midnight, I think. At least that's what I was told, I was pretty much out of it myself.'

'That's great, Abbey,' said Jo. 'I'll go to the hospital now. So just sit tight, yeah?'

Abbey nodded.

As Jo left, she sent in the family liaison officer, Cherry. 'Keep an eye on her, she's only just hanging on. Oh and make sure she sends through pictures of Damien to my mobile. We'll need them for a television appeal, but for God's sake don't tell her that.'

CHAPTER 41

'Hi, Abbey,' said Cherry as she entered Abbey's room. 'Did Jo tell you I was coming?'

Abbey managed a small nod. She was sat on the only sofa in the room, legs folded underneath her, picking at the cuff of her jumper.

There was an office chair sat at a desk and Cherry pulled it over. 'How are you doing? Do you think you could tell me?' she asked, taking Abbey's hands.

'How do you think I am? I'm a complete and utter wreck. I'm not eating, I am constantly crying and I wouldn't wish this on my worst enemy.' Abbey was whispering, but the words flooded out of her as though pushed out of her mouth from somewhere deep inside her.

'Oh, Abbey, not knowing where your child is or how he is being treated is one of the hardest things to deal with. One minute you will feel a surge of hope, the next, a depth of despair that will threaten your very sanity. Life will become an emotional roller coaster that won't really stop until we've found Damien.'

Abbey nodded, tears streaming down her face.

'But there are things you must do. You must force yourself to eat and sleep. Your body needs food and sleep in order to endure this ordeal. Although eating and sleeping may seem incredibly difficult, you must try. If eating regular meals feels like too much just have healthy snacks. I'm here to help you with those. Why don't we make this sofa a place to relax and nap when you need to? I'll find you some cushions and a blanket. I'll make sure you are doing everything you can to take care of yourself. You need to be healthy for when Damien comes back.'

Abbey nodded. 'OK, if you say so. I'll try. I promise.' Her eyes were threatening to close and Cherry decided to take advantage of that.

'Look I've got some things here,' and Cherry grabbed a large bag she'd placed by the door. 'Here, put your head on this pillow.'

Abbey complied and as Cherry wrapped a blanket around her, Abbey grabbed her wrist and said, 'You'll wake me if there's any news?'

Abbey nodded. 'Of course, Abbey, I promise. I'll stay with you while you sleep, so you can let go now and rest.' She rubbed Abbey's back as the poor girl drifted off to sleep. Cherry's heart went out to her, what an awful thing to go through all on your own.

CHAPTER 42

'We might have a lead, Byrd. Come on,' Jo called as she left Abbey's house.

'Where are we off to, Boss?'

'The maternity ward at Chichester hospital. Abbey's just told me Edith was with her throughout the birth.'

Byrd grinned. 'Fingers crossed.'

'And toes,' said Jo.

Byrd drove to Chichester Hospital, as Jo gazed out of the window. Her earlier exuberance was draining away. This case was turning out to be a nightmare. It was no ordinary missing child case, that was for sure. Statistically speaking baby snatches were rare and were usually committed by women who had lost a child of their own and wanted a replacement, or who saw their own dead child in the snatched one. Either way, it was a mental health problem.

But not in this case. This was a malevolent being, wanting the child for himself. To... to do what? Jo had no idea.

Byrd burst out, 'This is bollocks. We have no real idea

who has Damien, where he is, or if he's even alive. It's terrifying!'

Jo could only agree. 'I know, Eddie,' she said. She alternated between feeling completely numb and totally terrified. 'I keep thinking how Damien must be feeling without his mother and the danger he is potentially in.'

Dark thoughts clouded her mind. If they didn't find the abducted child within the first 24 hours, odds were they wouldn't find him alive or ever find him, but she couldn't voice those thoughts. Refused to accept them, as if by ignoring them, they wouldn't be true.

Byrd pulled up in the hospital car park and turned the engine off. But he didn't make a move to get out of the vehicle. Instead he turned to Jo, 'Look if Edith and the Watcher aren't, well what I mean is... is it possible that they aren't...'

'Aren't human? Is that what you're suggesting, Eddie?'

Byrd coloured and tapped his fingers on the steering wheel. Taking a deep breath he said, 'Well, yes, I suppose that is what I'm saying. What about you?'

Jo smiled, but it was a watery one. 'I know Edith and the Watcher are not human. They can't be. There were no pictures of Edith on Abbey's phone, remember? I didn't challenge Abbey on it, but I'm sure it wasn't a case of camera failure.'

Byrd took her hand and squeezed it, but Jo thought it was more to reassure himself than her. Either way she was glad of his touch.

'Come on, we can't stay in here all day. Let's try the hospital. See if we can find anyone who may have met Edith.'

She wasn't at all sure they would, but nothing ventured, nothing gained. In the meantime, as she stole a glance at Byrd, his words were a turn up. Maybe, just maybe, he was beginning to acknowledge that there were things that defied rational explanation in this world. That they lived in a world where the fabric of the divide between the living and the dead sometimes had a tear in it. And who knew what monsters had slipped through.

As they walked, Jo shivered and pulled her coat collar up around her neck. She hated winter. The cold dark nights kept people off the streets. Leaving them empty. Creating a void that was filled with things that lived in the shadows. Evil beings like the Watcher and his acolytes who came out to play while the world was covered by the blanket of the night, muffling sight and sound.

She groped for Byrd's hand and grabbed it. He moved closer and as their shoulders touched, she drew strength and comfort from his presence.

CHAPTER 43

Arriving at the ward, they talked to the sister in charge, Helen Cross, and explained that they needed to talk to the midwives that were on duty on the 31st October. Halloween. Cross called for the midwives who were on duty, one by one. But all their answers were negative. None of the midwives remembered Edith or Abbey.

Sister Cross suggested they check with records to find out who else was on shift that day. 'Sorry but we can't really remember last week never mind the last three months, all the mothers and babies tend to blur into one.'

'This was a big baby, though,' said Byrd.

'Oh? Really? Well that might help jog memories.'

'The baby was a boy, over 10 lbs with a shock of black hair.'

At last they got a reaction. 'Oh I heard about him,' she said. 'I wasn't here though, and I don't know who was. Like I said you'll have to speak to records.'

Sister Cross gave them directions to the administration offices and Byrd and Jo went to ask for the information they needed.

'Sorry,' said an officious receptionist. 'We can't just give out information like that.'

'But we've told you, this is about a missing child,' Jo said.

'I'm very sorry I'm sure, but policy is clear. We can't release any information on staff without a Warrant.'

'But that might take a couple of days!' Jo blurted. 'We can't wait a day, never mind several. We need this information now! What is wrong with you people? Don't you care?'

'Jo,' murmured Byrd and took her arm, leading her away from the receptionist. 'Calm down, that's not helping, come on, deep breaths.'

Jo did as she was asked. After a moment she said, 'Sorry, Eddie, but we need to find Damien and no one seems to care!'

'That's not true, the whole team care.'

'Yes, sorry, I know they do. It's just with everything else going on, I'm not sure how much longer I can cope or how much more I can take.' For once Jo was brutally honest with Byrd. She was no longer speaking as his superior officer, but as his lover and friend.

He rubbed her arm. 'I know, look go and wait in the car, let me handle this,' and he handed her the keys.

She nodded and turned away. She was aware she hadn't been necessarily talking about how much more she could take with the case, but really about her relationship with Byrd. She walked away before he could say anything else. She was still clinging to the hope that they could get through the blockage in their relationship. But the indecision had been going on too long. He seemed to still need her as he thawed every now and again, but then rapidly retreated. She sniffed back tears.

She still had to continue to hope. If his decision was that he couldn't carry on their relationship because of her gift, she didn't want to hear it, ever, because then there really would be no hope and she needed that hope to keep her going.

But she was very emotional about this case, she knew that. What on earth was wrong with her? Did she secretly want a child of her own? Was she becoming broody? How would that work then? Because she couldn't have children. That was the other elephant in the room. Even if Byrd finally, totally, accepted Jo for who and what she was, he didn't know that she was barren. That she didn't have functioning reproductive organs. Specifically ovaries. She'd been told that IVF could be a course of action with donor eggs, but its success couldn't be guaranteed and was very expensive. She wasn't sure she'd be able to go through all that. Anyway, that was a long way off. The more immediate problem was that Eddie didn't know. Not that she even knew if he wanted children. The whole thing was a subject best left alone.

She reached the car and clambered in. Turning on the engine, she set the heating up to high. Once on her own, without spectators, she burst into tears and sobbed. Letting all the hurt, and more importantly, her fear for the future, drain out of her.

Byrd joined her 15 minutes later. By then she'd stopped bawling like a child, or a lovesick teenager, and was once more composed.

'Well?' she asked as he climbed in the car.

'We've found the midwives who were working on the 31st October and their contact details are being emailed over as we speak.'

'And CCTV?'

'They're sending over the files for the day Abbey

arrived so we can go over them. Also if Abbey gives her consent, they will release her medical records about the birth.'

Jo relaxed. 'I don't know how you managed that, and to be honest I don't care. Thank you.'

Byrd put the car in gear, and they headed back to the police station in silence. Each wrapped up in their own thoughts. Jo desperately wanted to read Byrd's mind, but couldn't. Her gifts didn't extend to mind reading, a thought which made her smile. But once more, nothing had been said about the state of their relationship.

CHAPTER 44

By the time Jo and Byrd returned to the station, Sasha had received the information from the hospital. They had sent over the staff rota for 31st October and the contact details for them all. Jo immediately put Jill and Ken on that task, to start trying to trace them and speak to them. The two questions were: do they remember Abbey and the baby, which was a boy and unusually large, and did they meet Edith?

But at the end of a very long and frustrating session on the phones, all they found out was that people remembered Abbey and her son, but no one remembered Edith. She wasn't there at all are far as the midwives and auxiliary staff were concerned. Neither could she be found on CCTV from inside the hospital. Sasha found Abbey being dropped off at the entrance to the hospital in what looked like a Ford Fiesta. But she couldn't identify the colour of it, as the footage was black and white. They couldn't see the registration number either, as the number plate was covered in mud and dirt.

And so they had absolutely nothing that could lead

them to Edith. Jo walked into her office and Eddie followed her.

'So who the hell has the baby?' Byrd asked. 'Can it be this Edith who doesn't show up on CCTV and whom no one can remember? Is she even real?'

'She is to Abbey. She sews clothes for her and then Abbey sells them for goodness sake.'

'But we have absolutely no idea where she is now,' said Byrd.

Jo sat down in her chair with a thump. 'Well wherever Edith is, I hope she's looking after the baby. The thought of an evil being watching the child, well it doesn't bear thinking about.'

CHAPTER 45

Abbey woke with a start. Where was she? What time was it? Fingers of sunlight were filtering through the curtains. Crikey it must be morning, she realised, and she'd been asleep on the sofa. She pushed the blanket off her and sat up, just as Cherry came into the room carrying two mugs.

'Oh, hi. I've made us a hot drink. Tea without sugar, isn't it?' and she handed Abbey a mug, with 'The World's Greatest Mother' splashed on it. Abbey's hand started to shake and Cherry had to quickly grab the drink off her.

'How have I slept so long?' Abbey wailed 'How could I have slept while Damien is missing? What sort of mother am I? This whole thing must be my fault!'

Cherry put down her own drink and moved to sit next to Abbey on the sofa.

'Oh, Abbey, don't blame yourself. I know you must feel that there was something you could have done to have prevented Damien's disappearance, but it's just not true. You can literally drive yourself crazy asking, what if? If you didn't arrange for his disappearance, you shouldn't hold yourself responsible for not knowing or doing something that may seem obvious in hindsight. You couldn't have known what would happen when Edith took Damien for a walk. It was something she often did, wasn't it?'

Abbey nodded but wasn't appeased. 'I am to blame,' she insisted.

'No, Edith is to blame. Don't shoulder the blame of others, that way lies madness.'

'But what must people think of me?'

'Oh, Abbey, if some do blame you, it's only because they are projecting their own fears for their children, onto you. Blaming you makes them feel somewhat safer in the world because they hold you -- and your supposed mistake -- responsible for your child's abduction, rather than the abductor. Thinking about the abductor makes the crime real, which in turn makes the abductor real and therefore they think that that person could come and snatch their own child. It's an avoidance tactic, nothing more. You're a wonderful mother, Abbey and don't let anyone tell you otherwise. Now come on, get that hot drink inside you and then maybe try and eat a little toast.'

CHAPTER 46

Edith looked down at the child. She wasn't happy. Being a de facto mother wasn't one of her life goals, or even undead goals, but the Watcher had insisted and what he wanted, went. Children looked so contented when they slept, she thought. But Damien was sleeping less and less as he grew. Already acting like a toddler at just three month's old and clad in age one clothing, he was set to become a giant among men. A goliath. Undefeatable and indestructible. If he inherited his father's power, then... Edith turned away from visions of death and destruction.

She did feel a bit sorry for Abbey, mind. The poor girl had been through a lot and... but Edith didn't finish that thought, she didn't do compassion. She heard noises outside, scuffing of feet, suppressed laughter and rustling of clothes. Inching back the curtain, she peered out of the window. It was just a couple passing. Nothing to worry about. She turned back from the window and yelped in surprise.

'Will you stop doing that!' she exploded at the Watcher. 'Keep appearing without any warning. You'll be the death of me.' Then she laughed, for she was already dead.

But the Watcher didn't join in with her mirth. He never did. He was curmudgeonly; a bad-tempered devil if ever she saw one.

'So what happens now?' Edith asked.

'You take care of Damien until he's of an age when he can fend for himself.'

'Me?'

'Yes, you. Why? Do you have plans?'

The Watcher began rippling, a prelude to anger if ever she saw one. The air thickened. It was becoming difficult to breathe. His hands snaked around her neck, his talons digging into her flesh. She was lifted into the air, her body limp as she was shaken like a rag doll. Trying to speak, her mouth opened and closed, until she managed to let out a strangled, 'No!'

She was released and fell to the floor. 'Good. Now we understand each other.'

Edith nodded, got to her feet, patted her hair back into place and adjusted her clothing. She was going to have to be careful. The Watcher wasn't known for his benevolence. She knew he'd banish her on a whim and shivered at the thought of going back to Damnation. No, this was a much better gig. She'd stick with it as long as she could.

She had a lot of questions, but daren't ask them. What was the Watcher going to do with Damien? What was he training him to be? The embodiment of the Watcher on earth? After all he was the Watcher's son. It was safe to assume he would continue to do his father's work. He would be needed to ensure the continuation of the bloodline.

But she couldn't help wondering if certain humans

would rise up to battle the threat the Watcher and Damien posed. When a smaller, weaker opponent would face a much bigger, stronger adversary. She knew all about the story of David and Goliath. But just because David won then, didn't mean that his mother and her cohorts would win now.

But the niggling doubt remained.

CHAPTER 47

Osian had tossed and turned most of the night and he got up with the rising sun, unable to rest. Round and round in his head went the messages left behind at Halloween, including the one when Damien had been taken. At the time, given the charged situation they found themselves in, Osian hadn't had much chance to consider the passages.

Making himself a strong coffee, he sat at his computer and pulled up the copy of the messages. The one he was particularly interested in said:

"I have begotten a strange son, different and unlike man, and resembling the sons of the God of heaven; and his nature is different and he is not like us, and his eyes are as the rays of the sun, and his face is glorious."

At last the penny dropped. It was a description of Noah, who built the ark and survived the flood sent to wipe out the Nephilim (children of the fallen angels and human women) and cleanse humanity of its impurities. He thought about that for a moment, then rang Jo. Engaged. He tried Jill. The call just rang and rang. No answer. Grabbing his coat, Osian set off at a run to the police station.

Out of breath and dishevelled, he asked the surprised policeman behind the screen for Jo Walsh.

'I don't think that will be possible, Sir. She's part of a very sensitive investigation at the moment. I am sure you can appreciate how busy she is.'

'She's looking for the missing child. I know that because I helped yesterday. Please tell her I'm here. Curate Osian Price from the Cathedral.'

'Very well, please take a seat.'

Osian couldn't sit and prowled around the reception area until Jill came bursting out of the door. 'Osian! What's the matter?'

'I think I know where Damien is.'

'Really? Oh my, God! Oh, sorry, sorry, come on!' and she pulled at his arm.

Jo made everybody calm down. Sasha made coffee, everyone was forced to sit and only then was Osian allowed to explain.

'I've been thinking about the message left at Storm's house on Halloween from the Watcher. Well, strictly speaking, the message is the description of Noah at his birth. I think the Watcher used it to show how special his own son is.'

'Noah? Isn't that something to do with the floods?' asked Byrd.

'Yes. In the bible Noah has to build an arc to survive the floods. So maybe they are on a boat. The Watcher wants to survive with his son. And he could be using the analogy that the safest place for his only son would be on a boat.'

'But why? Isn't that a bit of a stretch?' Jo said.

Osian ploughed on, desperate for them to understand. 'No, because on a boat they could sail away until the time is right to return, when Damien is grown. Don't you see? Then Damien can be let loose on the world, to procreate with human women and keep the bloodline going. Just as Noah was the saviour of mankind, so Damien will be the saviour of the Watcher's lineage. And if God tries to wipe him off the face of the earth, he could weather the storm on a boat. He could also hide very effectively on the rivers and canals.'

'Sasha, get a large-scale map,' said Jo. 'Let's take a look at where on the coast he could be.'

'There's a bloody lot of water around here,' said Byrd.

'I know that, come one think, Eddie, think,' she urged.

'Would they be in the marina?'

'I'm not sure about that one,' said Jill. 'It could be too busy. People would notice them there and talk. Presumably they've taken a boat that's empty, moored up but not being used. There are loads of fair-weather sailors who don't use their boats from one month to the next in the marina and so anyone messing about out one would attract attention.'

'I agree,' said Jo. 'It needs to be somewhere quiet. Where they won't be noticed.'

'The Cathedral,' said Osian. 'The Watcher seems fascinated by it.'

'Sorry? What's that got to do with it?' said Eddie sounding dismissive. 'You're losing me, Osian.'

'Well, the way I see it is that you are never far from the Cathedral in Chichester. It dominates the skyline and can even be seen from the sea. So if we want somewhere on water, but quieter than the marina, within sight of the Cathedral...'

'The canal,' shouted Jill, then blushed. 'Sorry.'

'No, you're right,' said Jo. 'That makes sense. A houseboat on the canal. Perfect. Sasha, where's the main body of houseboats?' confident that Sasha, the font of all knowledge would know without looking it up.

'On the stretch of canal running alongside the marina, there are about 30 berths for houseboats.'

'So what now?' Osian looked around expectantly. 'Do we go in?' He was aware he was speaking from watching too many crime shows.

'Softly, softly,' said Jo. 'We go house to house.'

'Or boat to boat,' quipped Eddie.

CHAPTER 48

Jo was rather enjoying the romantic stroll with Byrd along the tow path. Unfortunately there was an undercurrent. They were there on an operation and not for love. Still, hanging onto Byrd's arm felt good.

Jo and Eddie were walking one way and Jill and Osian the other, and they were hoping to meet up at a houseboat that contained Damien, whichever one that might be. Fingers crossed it would work and not be a colossal waste of time and resources that could have been used to comb the city for the baby.

There were no other police visible. Back-up and an ambulance were waiting in a nearby car park out of sight of the canal, with Ken. They didn't want to warn the Watcher of their presence.

Surprisingly, Sykes had agreed to their operation and didn't veto it. But there was something off about that. The gleam in his eye didn't seem to be from excitement that they were very close to finding Damien. More a hardened cynical stare that said it would be Jo's fault if anything went wrong, and he'd actually enjoy seeing her squirm if it did. She was beginning to understand that that was how Sykes worked. If there was someone he wanted to get rid of, he usually gave them enough rope to hang themselves and then denied all knowledge of the operation. Jo hated sneaky people and according to Mick, Sykes was one of the sneakiest. Still, no matter, Jo would find Damien with or without Sykes.

They were about halfway down the line of houseboats when they heard a baby cry. Lingering, they kissed and waited until Jill and Osian were within hearing. She was rather enjoying snogging Byrd, and she was beginning to feel like a teenager. He was responding in kind and she wondered if Byrd was acting, or if his feelings were real. Could the conclusion of this case be the breakthrough they'd been waiting for both professionally and personally? It's what Jo wanted more than anything.

Jill and Osian were doing the same from the other end of the canal. Walking along, holding hands, just a loving couple out for a walk.

Then Osian stopped walking. 'Jill, I...'

'What are you doing? Osian, what is it?'

'Um, I hope I'm not jumping the gun here.'

'Gun? What gun? What are you talking about?'

'No, not literally. I mean I hope I'm not speaking too soon, or out of turn. But, well, I wanted to say that the more I see you and talk to you and spend time with you, well the more I want to do it,' he blushed.

'Oh, Osian, shut up,' said Jill and promptly kissed him full on the lips. 'There, that's all you had to do,' she whispered and they kissed again. Then Jill remembered where they were. 'Stop. First the baby, then the kisses. OK?'

'OK,' said Osian and smiled, feeling that despite the desperate situation they found themselves in, he'd never been happier.

CHAPTER 49

Once the two couples stopped at either end of the same houseboat, one practically in the middle of the stretch of towpath, they once again could hear a baby cry.

'So where are you taking me for my birthday?' Jo asked Byrd.

'It's a surprise,' he replied.

They were the code words for armed response to mobilise and storm the boat. Jo had wondered about evacuating the boats either side, once they'd identified their target boat. But had decided against it, as that could alert the Watcher and Edith, and they could have fled with the child, evading capture. As it happened, the boats either side of their target were quiet and seemed locked up tight.

A voice came over her earpiece, 'Understood, moving in.'

It was a matter of minutes until the armed response team silently approached from both ends of the canal. At an instruction from the team leader, they jumped aboard and broke through the houseboat door, shouting,

'Armed police, hands up, hands up, armed police!'

The two couples could only stand and watch and wait.

Jo was holding her breath. She really needed to find Damien and return him to his mother. She was mumbling under her breath, 'Please, please, come on,' when she heard a baby cry. Her relief was so great, it made her go weak. She buckled, but Byrd caught her and held her up.

Then she felt a beating at the air, it surrounded them, hovering like a helicopter, wings like rotor blades chopping through the air. It was the Watcher. Jo was sure of it, looking like a black cloud, with a storm of flies around it. The air became frigid and she shivered. She felt a pressure in her head. Someone or something was trying to invade her mind. Trying not to panic she put up a mental barrier. It was as though a bird was repeatedly flying into a window and bouncing off the glass, trying to get inside the house. She kept the pressure up, determined not to allow the Watcher into her head. She heard his frustrated roar, filling her head with a maelstrom of noise. She put her hands over her ears, but it didn't help as the noise was inside her head. Finally, he gave up.

He took off and Jo heard, 'Catch me if you can!'

She wasn't sure if the words were spoken aloud or were in her head. Looking up to the sky, she saw the black mass merge with the clouds and dissipate.

She leaned against Byrd, exhausted, her mind still confused from the battering it had just taken.

'Catch me if you can?' asked Byrd.

So maybe the Watcher had said the words out loud. He was throwing down the gauntlet for a fight. But elsewhere, not where they were.

'What the hell,' said Osian. 'Was that who I think it was?'

Jill nodded. 'I reckon that was Azazel, the fallen angel, the Watcher.'

'Osian,' Jo called. 'Where would he go?'

'The Cathedral.'

Of course.

'Ken,' Jo said as she spied him stood on the back of the houseboat. 'Take Damien to the ambulance for a check over and call Cherry, give her the good news and get her and Abbey to meet you here.'

'Where are you going?' Ken shouted.

'The Cathedral,' said Jo and they hurried away.

'Why there?' asked Byrd as they moved away from the boat.

'Because of the gargoyles,' said Osian. 'They are demons who were forever forbidden to enter the church. This demon will be no exception. He was once an angel. But is one no more in the sight of God, his father. So he will be at the Cathedral wall, looking outward from the place he can no longer enter. We'll find him and he will be buried down among the dead where he belongs.'

Jo was relieved to hear the determination in Osian's voice. She was not alone in this struggle, Osian would be right beside her, his unshakeable faith in God giving him the strength to face the fallen angel.

CHAPTER 50

They approached the Cathedral with caution.

'Where would he go, Osian?' Jo asked.

Osian looked blank.

'Think, Osian, think,' Jo urged. 'With the living?' He shook his head. 'With the dead?'

'Of course,' said Osian. 'The dead live among the dead.'

He'd gone rather pale and Jo was afraid he wouldn't be strong enough to face the Watcher. This was a whole new experience for three out of the four of them. Jo had faced down two demons now and if she was honest enjoyed the fear, the faith in her strength and the encounters with Judith. Oh and the winning, of course. Which reminded her.

'Where's Judith?' The other three turned to look at her.

'Judith?' Byrd looked confused.

'Yes, she's always with me at times like this.'

'No,' Byrd said. 'Judith!' and he pointed over Jo's shoulder.

And there she was. Her best friend hadn't let her down. But they didn't have time for grand reunions.

She turned her attention to Osian. 'So if the Watcher goes among the dead, where in the cathedral would that be?'

'Paradise, the cathedral burial garden.'

'Right, Osian have you got your bible?'

'My what?'

'Your bible or Book of Enoch or whatever it is that you need to face the Watcher. Come on, Osian, stay with me,' she urged.

They ran to the Paradise Garden, a gated garden where the long dead lay. Everywhere was eerily quiet. There was no road noise, no people, night was drawing in and all were tucked up in their warm homes. They were isolated and alone. It felt as though they were the only ones left alive in Chichester.

Ice glistened on the railings. The temperature was falling, and Jo shivered in her coat. Was it just the night or something else? Whatever it was, the temperature was plummeting.

'He's here,' whispered Judith, suddenly appearing by Jo's side, making Jo jump.

'Bloody hell, Judith,' she hissed. 'I wish you wouldn't do that.'

Judith smiled not looking in the least sorry.

Jo glanced up at the sheer cathedral walls. She couldn't see the gargoyles in the growing gloom, but fancied she felt their eyes on her back. They made her skin crawl.

'Osian are you ready?' Jo called.

'What?'

'Your Book of Enoch!'

'Oh yes, sorry.'

'Chapter 10 start to read it as loud as you can!' Judith shouted to Osian.

The rush of air crept around them, softly at first, tugging at clothes, ruffling hair, blowing in ears, teasing, taunting.

'Don't be afraid,' shouted Jo to her little band of warriors. 'Don't be intimidated.'

Jo looked around. Osian was white and drawn. Jill looked scared out of her wits, holding onto Osian's upper arm and standing as close to him as she could. Judith looked implacable, serene even and Jo wondered how she managed that. Mind you, Judith was no longer human and had seen far more than they would ever know. She clearly believed they could beat the Watcher and therefore so should Jo. She stole a glance at Byrd, he managed a small smile, then turned his attention back to Judith, who was now standing at the front of their group, with the four of them in a line behind her.

The air became more turbulent. Whirled up in it were dead leaves, twigs and branches which struck them on the arms and shoulders. The leaves and mulch got stuck in her hair and clothes. As the wind rose, the noise rose. They were facing a hurricane, which buffeted them and rocked them, but they held their resolve. It could not dislodge any of them. Jo was proud of her ragged band.

'Osian,' she shouted. 'Start reading!'

She thought he read her lips rather than heard her.

She heard him begin: 'And again the Lord said to Raphael, bind Azazel hand and foot and cast him into the darkness and split open the ground and cast him in.'

Osian was halted by the sound of a million buzzing insects. Beating wings flew around them and he saw they were locusts. They flew into their hair, climbed in their ears, up sleeves, up legs and in shoes. Jill screamed and beat the air around her head. Osian grabbed her and pulled her to him so she could burrow her face and body into his chest. He clasped her to him with his arm. 'Stay strong,' he whispered in her ear. 'For I am with you sayeth the Lord. Trust in God and we shall prevail.'

He felt her nod her head. She didn't move from his arms, but he felt her body stiffen and straighten up.

With his free hand, he held the Book of Enoch and continued reading. 'And fill the hole by covering him with dark and jagged rocks, and cover him with darkness, and let him live there forever, and cover his face that he may not see the light.'

At once the locusts dropped to the ground. Some dead, some writhing in death throws and others still very much alive and crawling over their less fortunate brothers, began to eat them.

Osian wondered what else the Watcher was going to throw at them to try and stop them, but so far their band were unbroken, led by Judith, although Osian wasn't altogether too sure who she actually was. As the locusts were no longer filling the air, Jill lifted her head to make sure they were gone and then moved to stand by his side.

As the locusts fell to the floor, the air changed. The pressure increased; Byrd could feel it in his ears. He wanted to hold his nose and blow, to clear them, but couldn't. He had to keep his focus on the group and what Osian was saying. And then the air buffeted him this way and that, the noise of beating wings rang around the cathedral garden. Byrd was horrified as the fallen angel appeared in front of them. If he hadn't seen it with his own eyes, he'd never have believed it. The being hovered a few feet above the ground. He looked like the devil incarnate. Huge wings spread out from his back, magnificent in size, but with damage to them. Feathers were matted and dirty, some broken and others missing completely. His eyes were blackened, and skin peeled in strips from his face. He opened his mouth and beetles poured out of it. Hundreds, thousands, in a great stream that seemed never ending. They were scarab beetles, Byrd noticed, as they clacked along the floor and over each other in their desire to reach the group of believers. Byrd couldn't help it. He recoiled in horror. He couldn't take much more. And then Osian found his voice again.

'And on the great day of judgement he shall be hurled into the fire!' Osian shouted.

The beetles stopped.

'And on the great day of judgement, he shall be hurled into the fire!' Osian shouted again.

Judith straightened her arm, pointing at the beetles. From her finger streamed a bolt of fire, it was as though she were a human flame thrower. The flames licked over the mass of beetles and they caught fire. Jo recoiled from the heat as they exploded. Cooked and split bodies littered the ground and the wave of fire consumed them all. As they were still spewing out of the mouth of the Watcher, the flames hungrily consumed them, racing up the writhing stream of beetles, towards the Watcher himself.

Then Judith spoke. 'And on the great day of judgement, he shall be hurled into the fire!'

But it wasn't Judith speaking, Jo realised. There was someone standing in front of her friend. It was a beautiful figure. Not knowing how or why, Jo instantly knew it was the Archangel Raphael, who was set over all the diseases and all the wounds of the children of men. The great *healer of man and a particular enemy of the devil.*

His wings had an even greater span than the Watcher's and they were clean, groomed and gleaming. The feathers rippled as the wings moved. He was dressed in white with sandals on his feet fastened by thongs crisscrossing up his legs. Surrounded by a golden light Raphael advanced on the Watcher, who drew back, shrinking in size at each step the archangel took.

The four of them stood tall behind Raphael and Judith, and held hands. They seemed to grow in stature also, Jo noticed, as their combined faith played its part.

Jo, the gifted one, who believed in the spirit world and the good it could do.

Byrd, the sceptic, who would be forever changed by what he was witnessing.

Osian, the cleric, who's faith in God was a blazing light in the darkness.

Jill, the innocent, destined to be Osian's partner in life, who had a well of faith so deep it could never be emptied.

Jo felt a surge of energy as they all shouted: "And on the great day of judgement, he shall be hurled into the fire!'

In one last act of despair, the Watcher screamed out his rage and hatred, then burst into flames. The ground rumbled as a large fissure opened under his feet and the Watcher fell into it. With a grinding of rock on rock, the earth closed up and the fallen angel was sealed in his tomb.

Raphael turned to face them and they basked in the light of his blessing for a brief moment, before, his work done, he flew upward, back to the heavens. Judith turned to look at them and said, 'Thank you. Each and every one of you played your part. You will be changed by what you have witnessed tonight. We shall meet again.'

The four of them collapsed on the floor as Judith faded away and they were left alone in the Paradise Garden.

'Osian,' Jo said. 'Do you have anything to drink in your office? Preferably brandy?'

The young curate nodded and led the way as they picked themselves up and walked on unsteady legs, brushing detritus from their hair and clothes as they went.

CHAPTER 51

They stumbled into the Cathedral and onward into the warmth of Osian's office. Opening a cupboard, he quickly poured the golden liquid into four glasses and handed them around.

Jo, drained yet jubilant, raised her glass and said, 'Ready to fight another day!'

The others echoed her and drank. As the warmth of the liquid seeped through her, she embraced it and relaxed.

Byrd moved to her. 'Jo, I'm sorry for... for not believing in you, for not accepting you for who you are, for...'

'Shhh,' she said. 'It's alright.'

But he shook his head, 'No, it's not alright. But I'm here now, after all I can hardly deny what I've just seen with my own eyes, yet again! Especially as this time I played my part, not just watched from the shadows.'

She smiled, 'Thank you, you don't know how much that means to me.' Tears threatened, but she hid them with another sip of brandy.

'Osian,' she said. 'Are you OK?'

He nodded. 'A bit shaken, but OK thanks. I always believed there were evil beings, but seeing one? Well, that was a hell of an experience and one I don't want to go through again. At least until I've recovered from this one!'

They all smiled at his attempt at levity.

'And what about you, Jill?' Jo was a little concerned about her young DC, as she was the least experienced of their group.

'I'm just glad we could beat that, that, whatever he was.' Jill shuddered and took another drink.

Jo said, 'I think we emerged victorious tonight because of our combined faith in whatever it is that we believe to be true. And a big part of that is our belief in each other. Because we all believe in something other than evil, we were able to wage war against the fallen angel and win. Faith is the key. Belief is the key. Willingness to believe in something other. Something you have now seen with your own eyes even if you don't understand it.' Jo raised her glass a final time. 'To us,' she said and emptied her glass.

Placing it on Osian's desk she said, 'And now Byrd and I need to wrap up the case and go and make sure that Abbey and Damien are alright.'

CHAPTER 52

Jo was completing her paperwork in her office when Sykes walked in.

'Jo, a minute?' he said, closing her door behind him.

In the small space she felt intimidated. She was sat and he was standing, a role reversal that she didn't like. But it would look strange if she suddenly stood.

'Well done for finding the child. I take it all is well there?'

'Yes, Sir,' she said. 'He's been checked over and found to be unharmed. Both mother and child are back home.'

'And what about their future?'

'Abbey gave us an old address she had for Edith. We checked it out and it's a small 2-bedroom house that has been empty for years. Sasha has been onto the Housing Department and it transpires that as they were unable to trace the owner, they'd got a Possession Order and were refurbishing the property. Happily Abbey was top of the Housing List, so she's been allocated it and will be moving in soon. No more living in one room with Damien in a shared house. It should be ready in a week or so as the

Council have nearly finished the work.'

Sykes nodded his approval. 'And Edith?'

'Disappeared, Sir. There is a warrant out for her arrest, obviously.'

'So what exactly made you look at houseboats for the child?'

Jo was ready with the lie. 'Abbey told us how much Edith liked the canal and would often walk Damien along the tow path. It was a lead, when we had none, so we thought we'd follow that up.'

'Mmm,' Sykes looked sceptical. 'So, if I'm right, you've saved the day, but not caught the perpetrator - again! Am I right?'

'Well, if you put it like that...'

'I do, Jo, believe me I do. I'll be keeping a close eye on you and your team. One more move like this and you could find yourselves back on the beat.'

Sykes turned and stalked out of the room. It was then that Jo was glad she'd remained seated, her legs would have given way otherwise. His words were a shock. But, of course, on the surface, she supposed he was right. But his voice and words very much felt as though he didn't like her. Hated her, almost. She was concerned that if she didn't give him a guilty perpetrator on the next case, then he would ensure her small team would be disbanded. And he'd cover his own back by throwing her to the wolves.

CHAPER 53

Abbey was nothing short of ecstatic. She wandered around the small two bedroomed house she'd been given for her and Damien, and it came with a garden! She couldn't thank Jo and Byrd enough. They said that it was all the Housing Department and not them, but she wasn't having any of it.

She had a living room at the front of the house, running into a dining room at the back, with a small kitchen next to it. Upstairs there were two bedrooms. A large one for her and a smaller one for Damien. She was going to set up her office/work room in the dining space, so she had a view over the garden and would be able to watch Damien playing as she designed her clothes. She was thinking about bringing out a new line of children's clothing, she was so inspired by her son.

The doorbell broke through her thoughts. She had advertised for a new seamstress, now Edith was gone, and she'd had a reply already. A young woman who had taken the same sort of course that Abbey had and if they got on, they could have a real future together.

Abbey ran to the door and flung it open. A young girl stood there with the most striking silver hair. It fell to her shoulders in a long bob and framed her face, swinging, as she moved her head.

'Hi, I'm Abbey, please come in.'

The girl gave a smile and walked into the house. Abbey shut the door and following her, found her visitor in the dining room looking out over the garden. She turned, 'What a lovely home you have.'

Abbey returned the smile and thanked her.

'I'm so looking forward to getting to know you better,' the girl said. 'And your designs look amazing. I can't believe it, this is such a wonderful opportunity. You're so talented.'

Abbey grinned. Yes, this girl was someone she could work with. She instantly felt it. She felt she was familiar somehow. That they had an affinity. There was no denying or fighting it.

'I'm so sorry,' said Abbey. 'My mind's gone a complete blank and I've forgotten your name!'

The girl grinned. 'It Ed...' she cleared her throat. 'Sorry I meant to say Eve. My name is Eve.'

CHAPTER 54

Jo felt instantly at home. She was standing in the middle of the stable block at Homecroft Farm. She walked down past the stalls, petting each horse as she passed. They nibbled at her fingers, blew into her hands and brayed their welcome. A peace stole over her as she reached the last stall and the horse that would be her mount that day. Silver was a beautiful grey mare. She looked at Jo with placid eyes then pranced in excitement as Jo entered the stable and slipping on a headcollar led her outside. Once Silver was saddled and Jo kitted out, she climbed onto the horse's back

She'd not told her father, nor Byrd, about her visit as both of them would have tried to stop her. But she felt safe enough. She liked the woman who ran the stables and they were just going out for a quiet walk along the beach. She'd been longing to go for a ride for months and surely a quiet hack would be okay? She didn't need to go galloping over the downs.

With Bev leading the way they walked the short path to the beach where they led the horses to the shallows.

After checking Jo was still alright, Bev broke into a trot along the beach, with Jo following her. When they reached the end, by the cliffs, they stopped, facing outward to the sea.

Jo had loosened the reins, when suddenly Silver reared up in panic. Gripping with her knees and leaning over Silver's neck Jo managed to stay on. As Silver returned to standing on four legs, she took a better hold of the reins and looked out to sea.

The tumbling waves were foaming, and Jo wondered what had spooked the horse. Then she saw it.

An apparition was in front of her. Coming at her over the sea was a horse, rearing up on the foam. Its mane seemed part of the waves, its mouth was open, lips curled back to reveal rows of discoloured teeth, with wild staring eyes that seemed to look straight into her soul. Hooves clawed the air as it rode the waves like a surfer. The swell grew and tumbled, then crashed onto the beach and the horse was swallowed up by the mist.

Jo had heard of the legends surrounding horses. She'd read up on them when she was a girl and fascinated by all things horse. It could only be a Kelpie, a malevolent shape-changing aquatic spirit of Scottish legend.

If that were true, what the hell was one doing in Chichester?

THE END

Waking the Dead

Young men are disappearing from Chichester. Lured from their homes. Their bodies never found. But the last sightings were all near water. The families are furious with the lack of progress. They're out for blood. Jo's.

Book 4 in the Jo Wolfe Psychic Detective series is available from your local Amazon store.

By Wendy Cartmell

Sgt Major Crane crime thrillers:
Deadly Steps
Deadly Nights
Deadly Honour
Deadly Lies
Deadly Hijack
Deadly Widow
Deadly Cut
Deadly Proof

Crane and Anderson crime thrillers:
Death Rites
Death Elements
Death Call
A Grave Death
A Cold Death

Emma Harrison mysteries
Past Judgement
Mortal Judgement
Joint Judgement

Supernatural suspense
Gamble with Death
Touching the Dead
Divining the Dead
Watching the Dead
Waking the Dead

All my books are in KINDLE UNLIMITED and available to purchase or borrow from Amazon.

Check out my website and blog, where I review the very best in crime fiction.

wendycartmell.com

Happy reading
until next time…

Printed in Great Britain
by Amazon